A YOUNG BOY WALKS INTO
THE MYSTERIOUS BLACK FOREST . . .

. . . AND THE ADVENTURE BEGINS.

Graphic Spin is published by Stone Arch Books
A Capstone Imprint
151 Good Counsel Drive, P.O. Box 669
Mankato, Minnesota 56002
www.capstonepub.com

Library of Congress Cataloging-in-Publication Data

Tulien, Sean.

The golden goose : a Grimm graphic novel / retold by Sean Tulien ; illustrated by Thiago Ferraz.

p. cm. -- (Graphic spin)

ISBN 978-1-4342-2961-8 (library binding)

1. Graphic novels. [1. Graphic novels. 2. Fairy tales. 3. Folklore--Germany.] I. Grimm, Jacob, 1785-1863. II. Grimm, Wilhelm, 1786-1859. III. Ferraz, Thiago, 1987- ill. IV. Golden goose. English. V. Title.

PZ7.7.T85Go 2011

741.5'973--dc22

2010025195

Art Director/Graphic Designer: Kay Fraser

Summary: Simon is the neglected son of a poor woodcutter. Eliza is the bereaved Princess of a royal family. The two teens live separate lives, unaware of each other's existence — until a wild man from the mysterious Black Forest gifts simple Simon with a magical golden goose . . .

Printed in the United States of America in North Mankato, Minnesota.
092010
005933CGS11

A GRIMM GRAPHIC NOVEL



# The Golden Goose

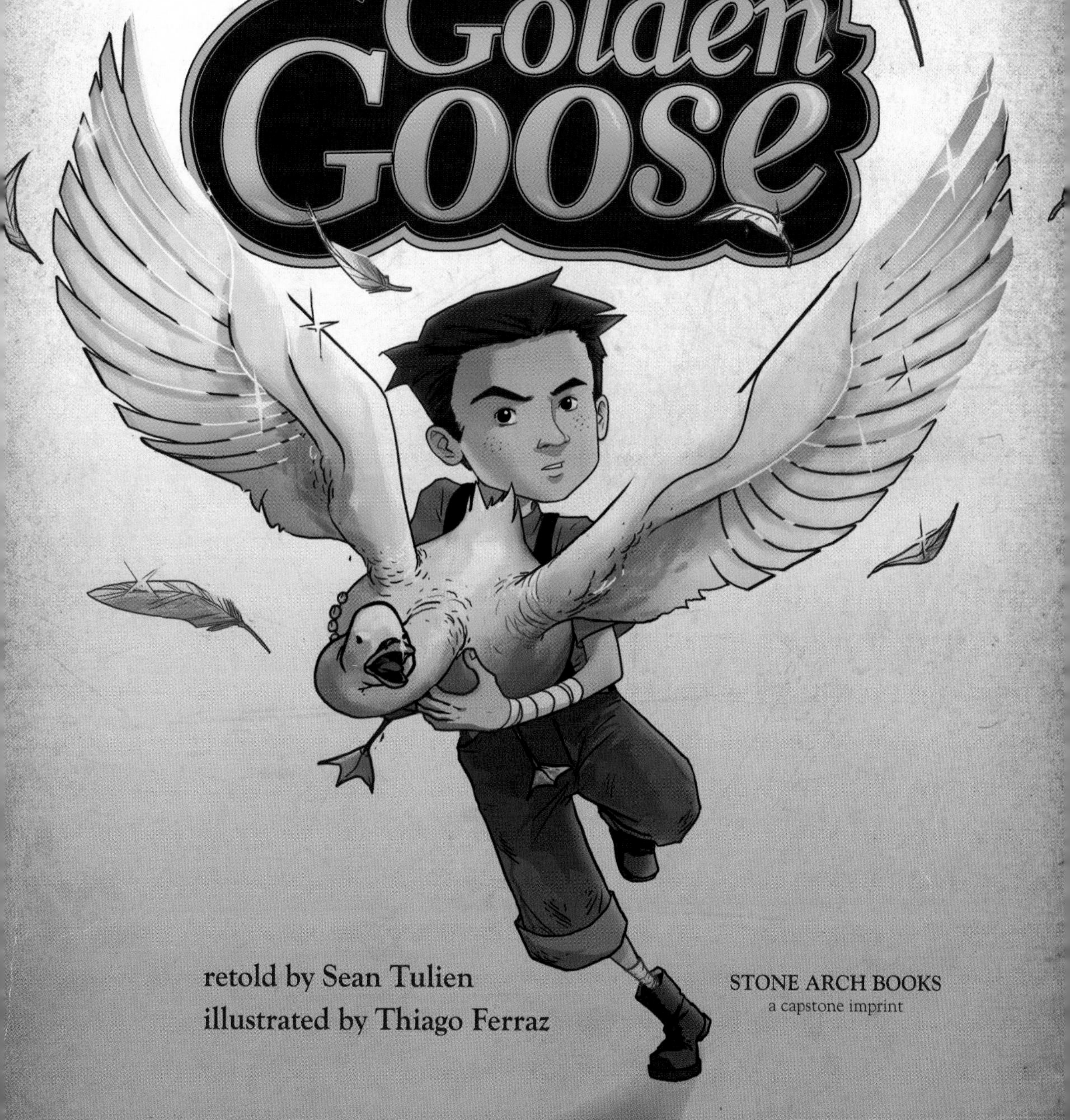

retold by Sean Tulien
illustrated by Thiago Ferraz

STONE ARCH BOOKS
a capstone imprint

# The Royal Court

The Queen

The King

Pierre the Court Jester

Princess Eliza

# The Black Forest

The Golden Goose

The Woodcutter

The Wild Man

Simon

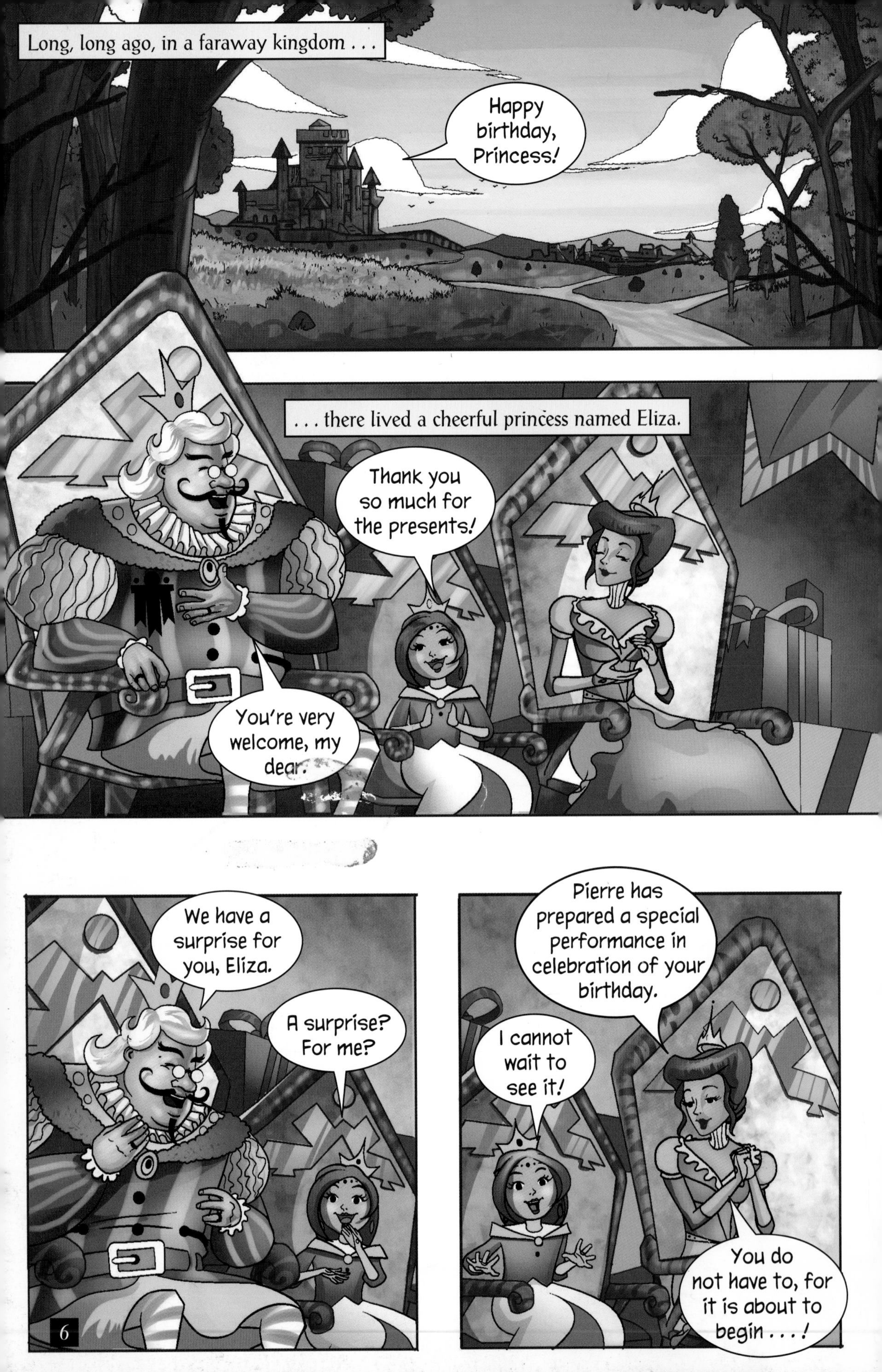
Long, long ago, in a faraway kingdom . . .
Happy birthday, Princess!
. . . there lived a cheerful princess named Eliza.
Thank you so much for the presents!
You're very welcome, my dear.
We have a surprise for you, Eliza.
A surprise? For me?
Pierre has prepared a special performance in celebration of your birthday.
I cannot wait to see it!
You do not have to, for it is about to begin . . . !

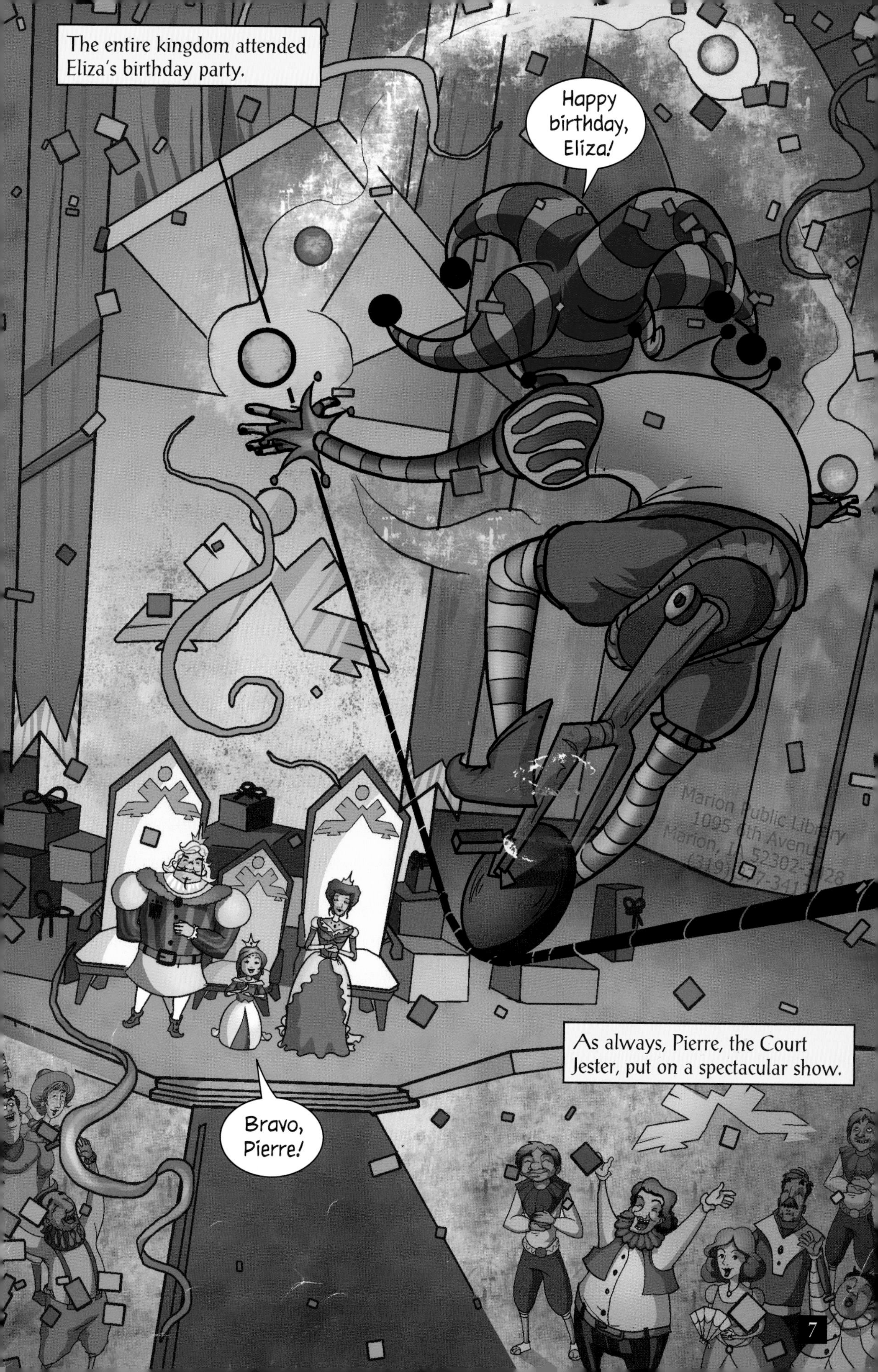
The entire kingdom attended Eliza's birthday party.
Happy birthday, Eliza!
As always, Pierre, the Court Jester, put on a spectacular show.
Bravo, Pierre!

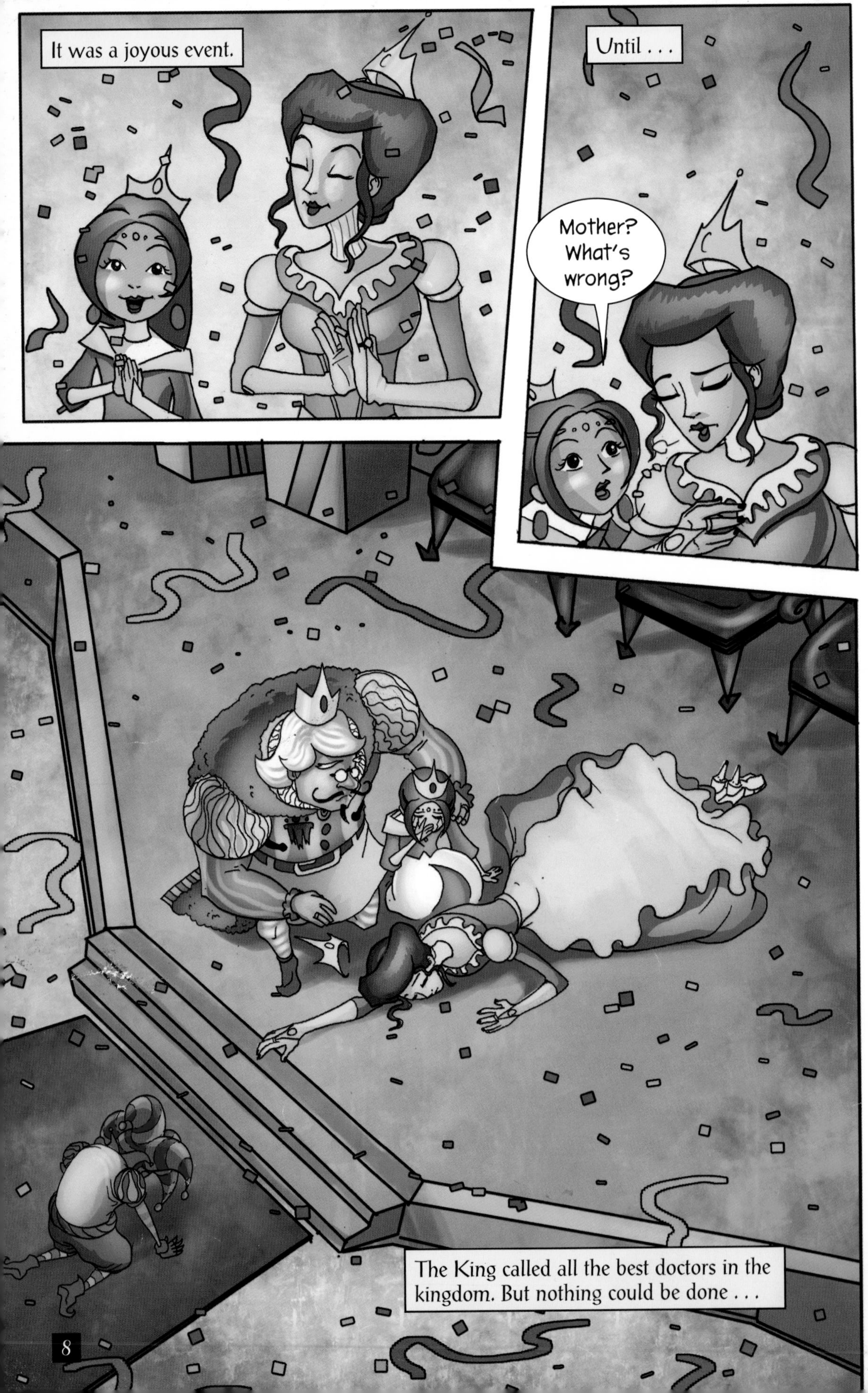
It was a joyous event.
Until . . .
Mother? What's wrong?
The King called all the best doctors in the kingdom. But nothing could be done . . .

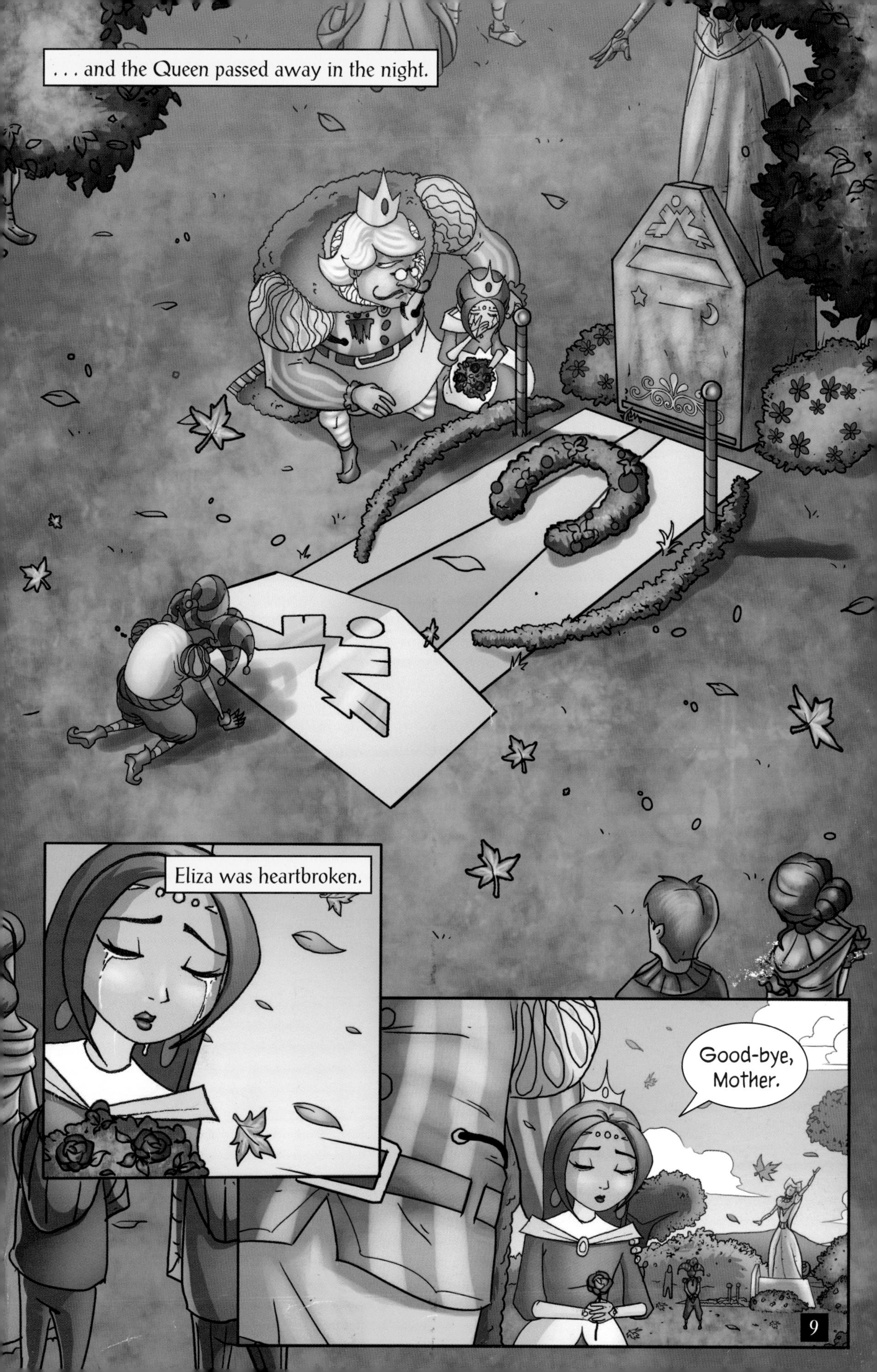
. . . and the Queen passed away in the night.
Eliza was heartbroken.
Good-bye, Mother.

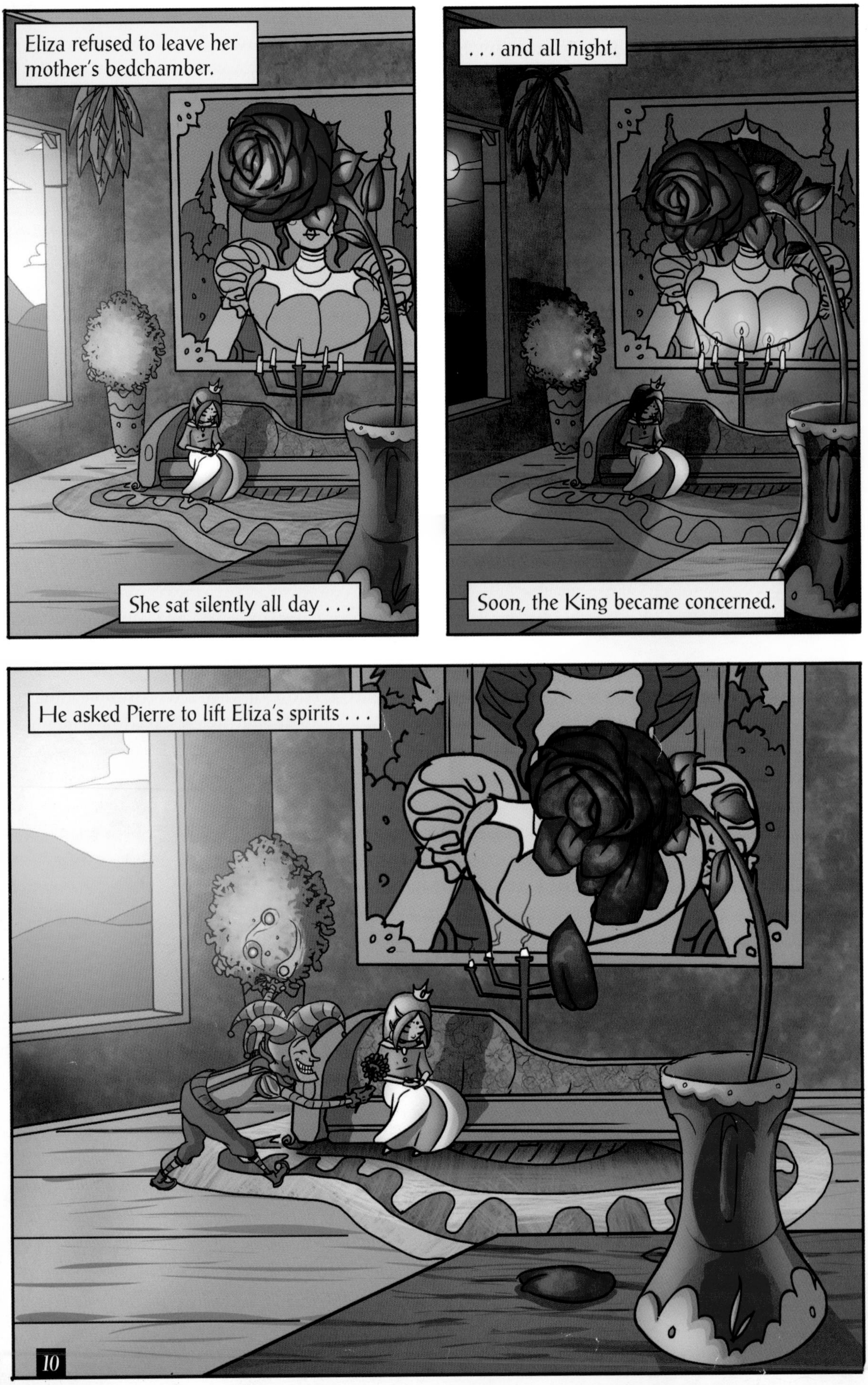

Eliza refused to leave her mother's bedchamber.
She sat silently all day . . .
. . . and all night.
Soon, the King became concerned.
He asked Pierre to lift Eliza's spirits . . .

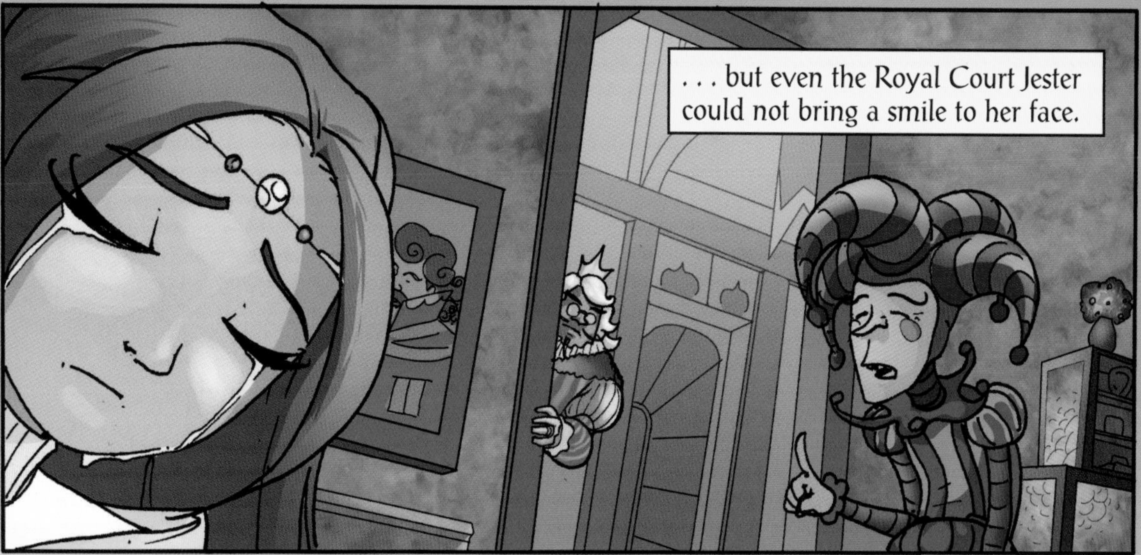
. . . but even the Royal Court Jester could not bring a smile to her face.

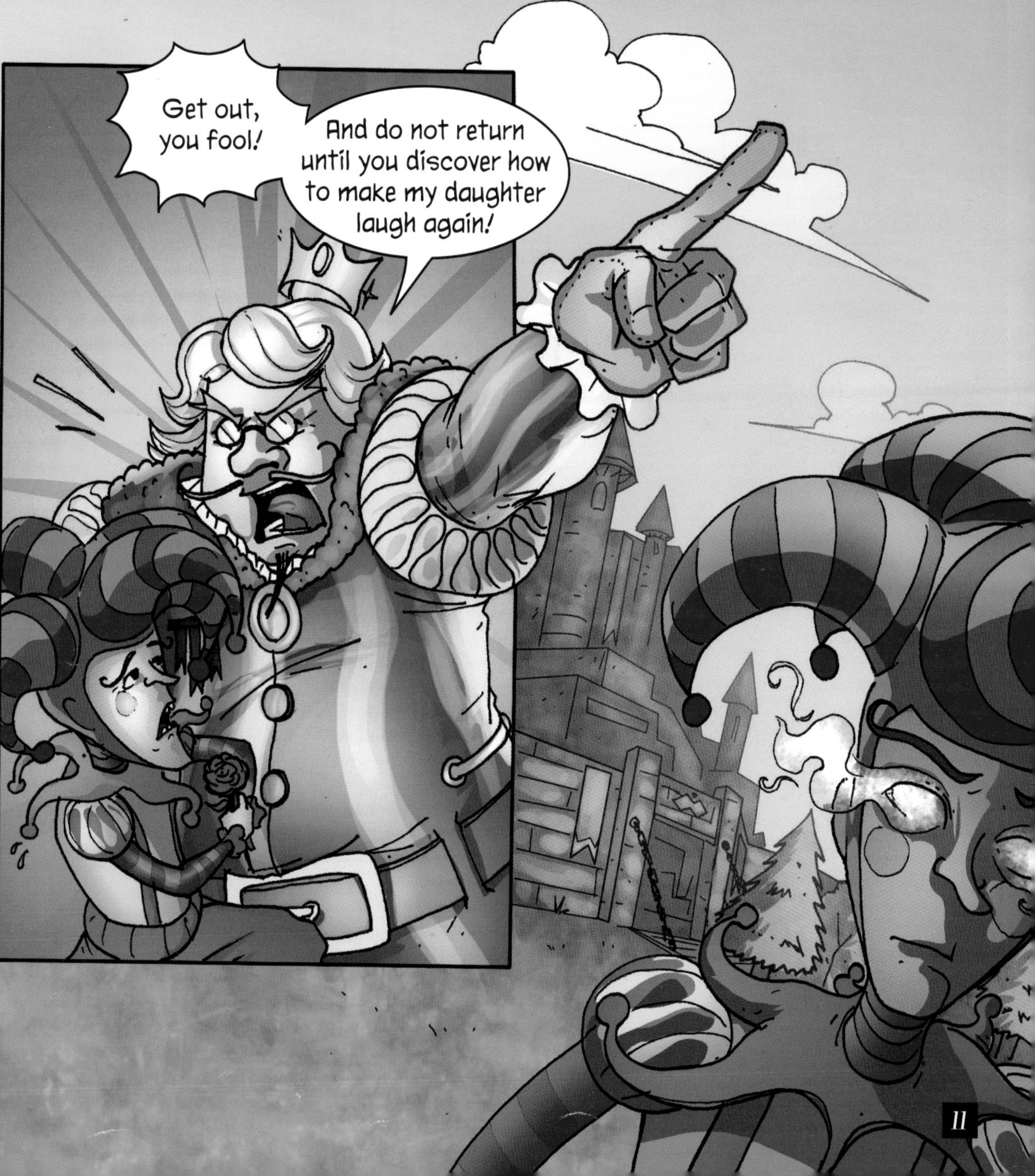
Get out, you fool!
And do not return until you discover how to make my daughter laugh again!

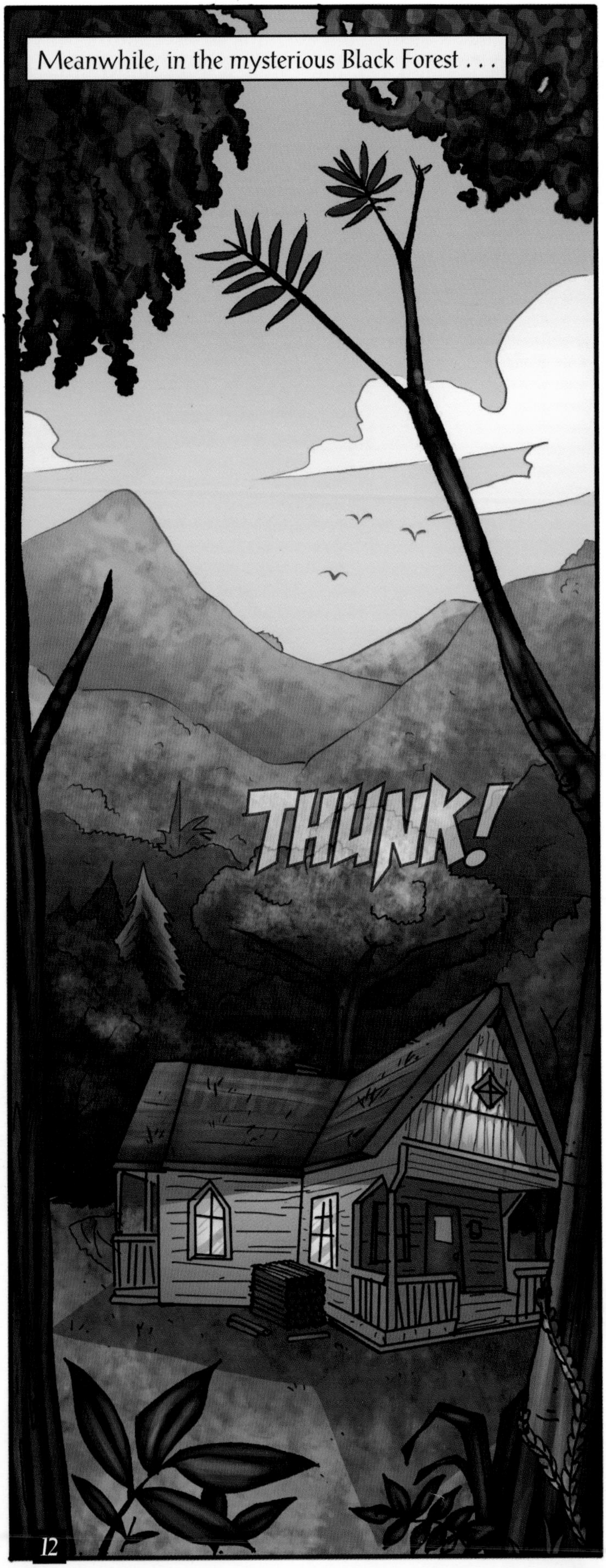
Meanwhile, in the mysterious Black Forest . . .
THUNK!

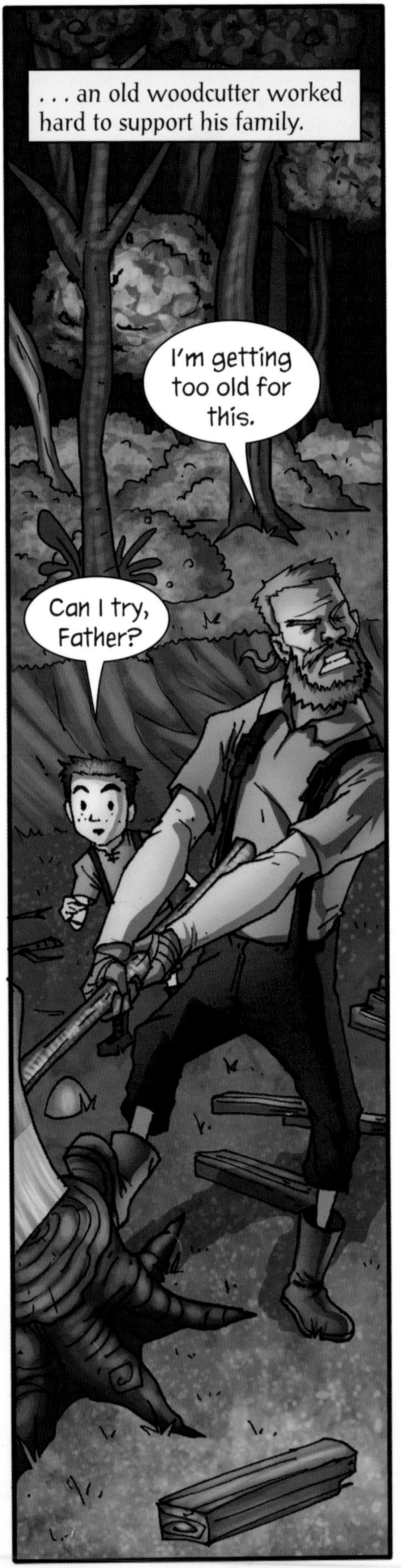
. . . an old woodcutter worked hard to support his family.
I'm getting too old for this.
Can I try, Father?

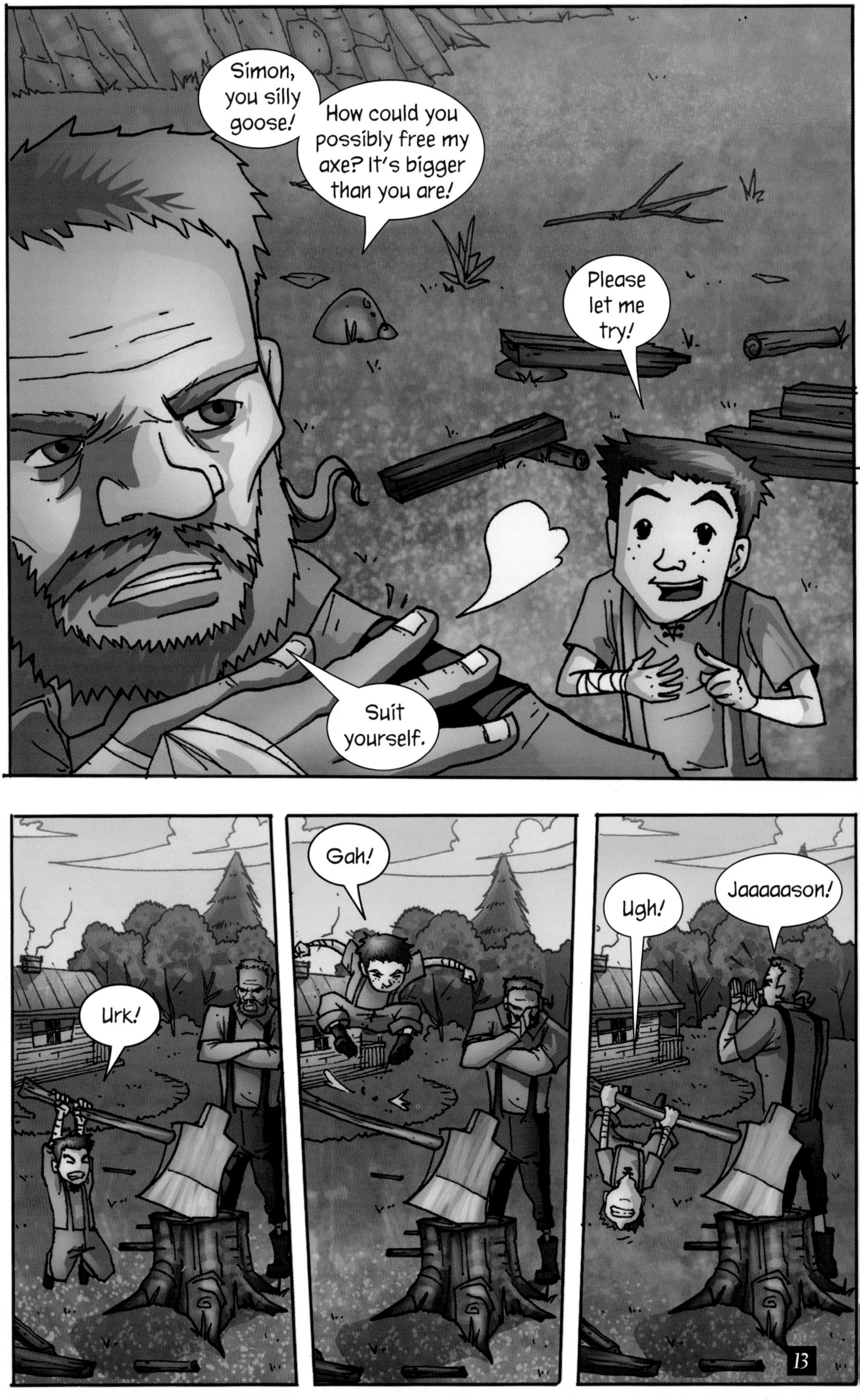
Simon, you silly goose!
How could you possibly free my axe? It's bigger than you are!
Please let me try!
Suit yourself.
Urk!
Gah!
Ugh!
Jaaaaason!

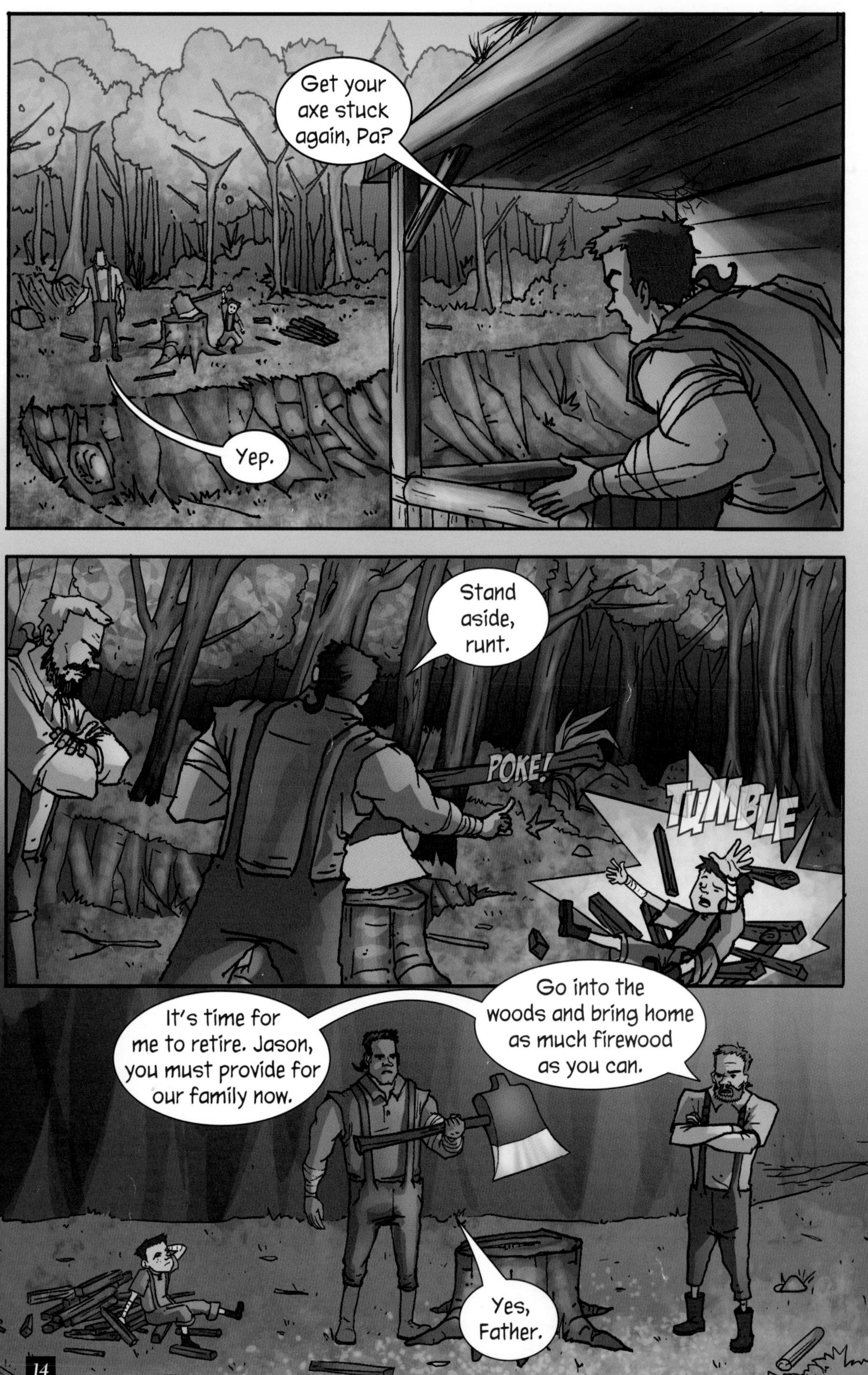
Get your axe stuck again, Pa?
Yep.
Stand aside, runt.
POKE!
TUMBLE
It's time for me to retire. Jason, you must provide for our family now.
Go into the woods and bring home as much firewood as you can.
Yes, Father.

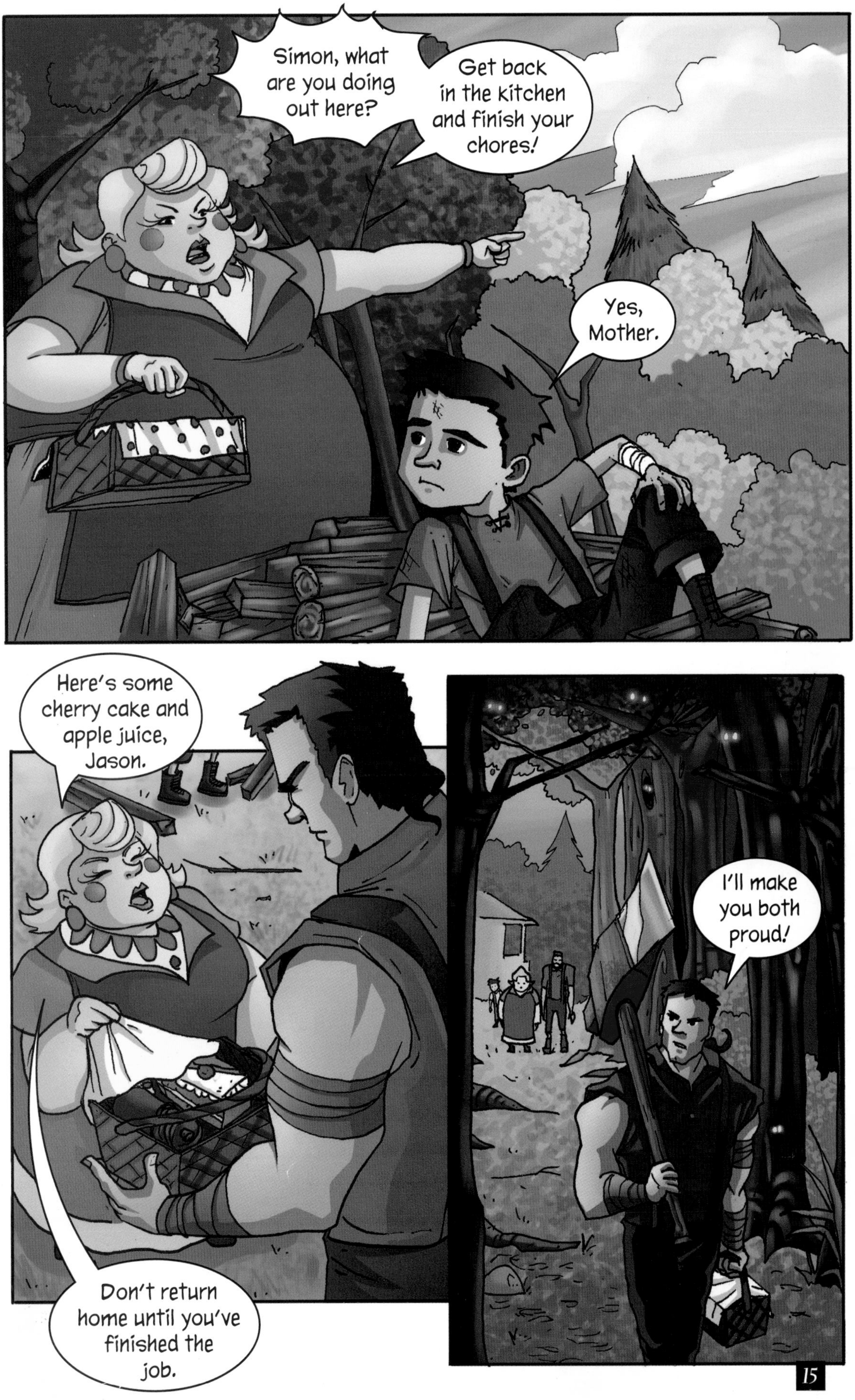
Simon, what are you doing out here?
Get back in the kitchen and finish your chores!
Yes, Mother.
Here's some cherry cake and apple juice, Jason.
Don't return home until you've finished the job.
I'll make you both proud!

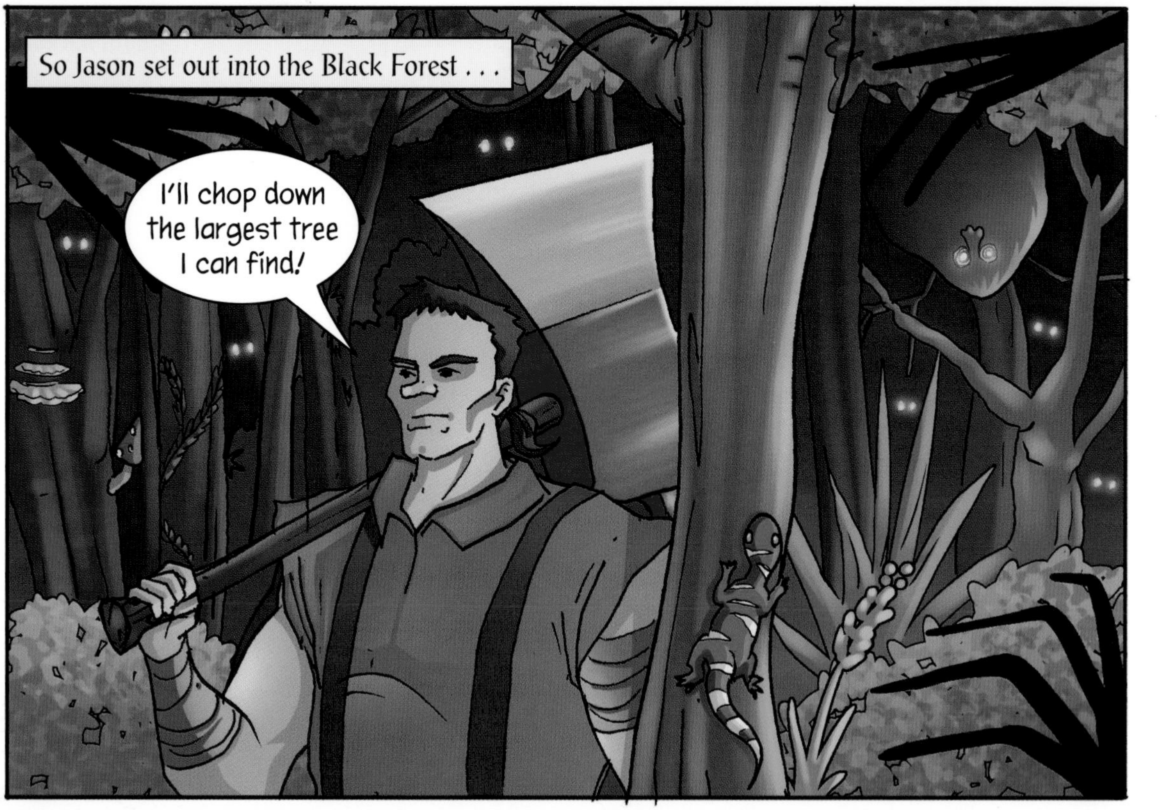
So Jason set out into the Black Forest . . .
I'll chop down the largest tree I can find!

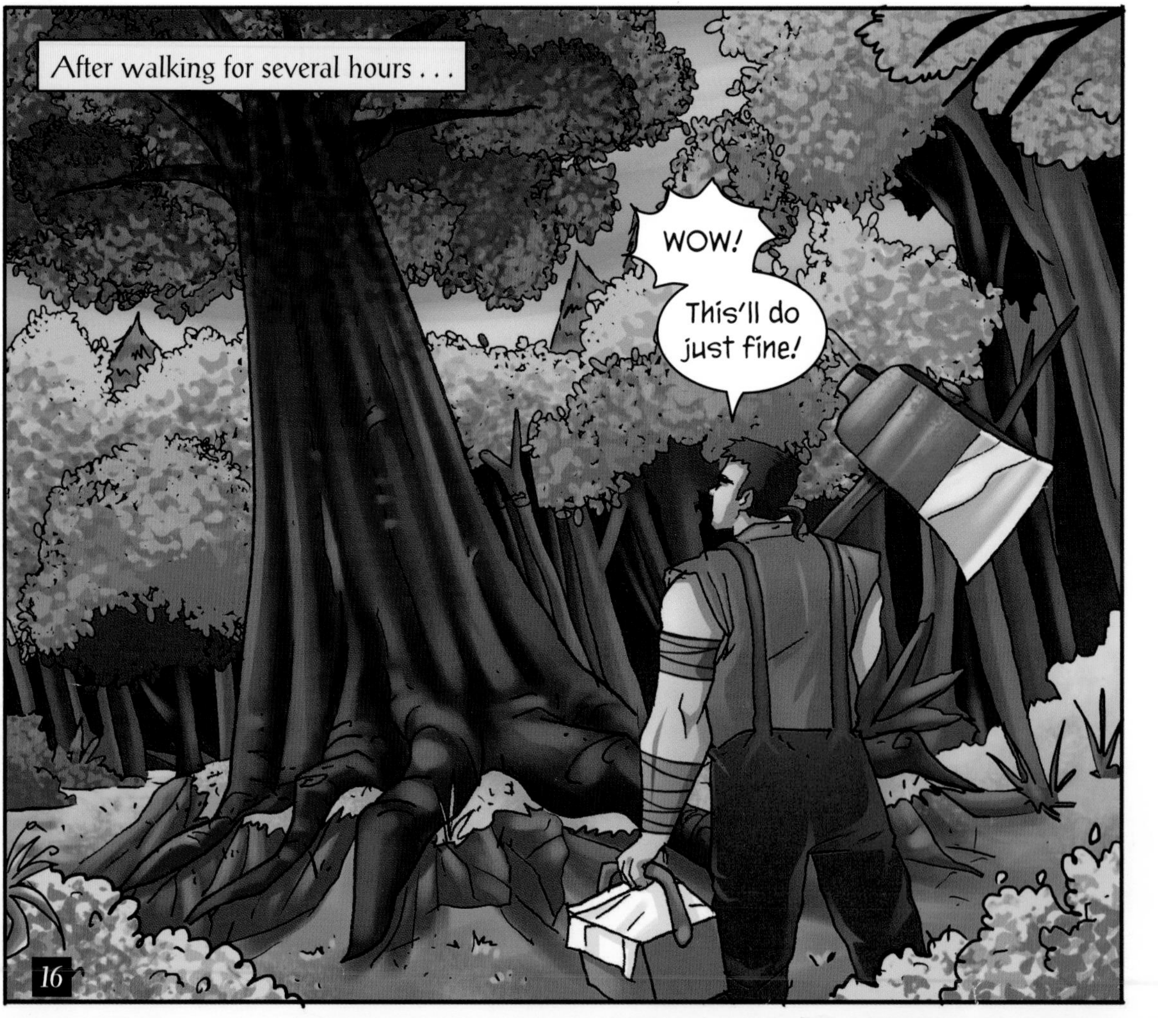
After walking for several hours . . .
WOW!
This'll do just fine!

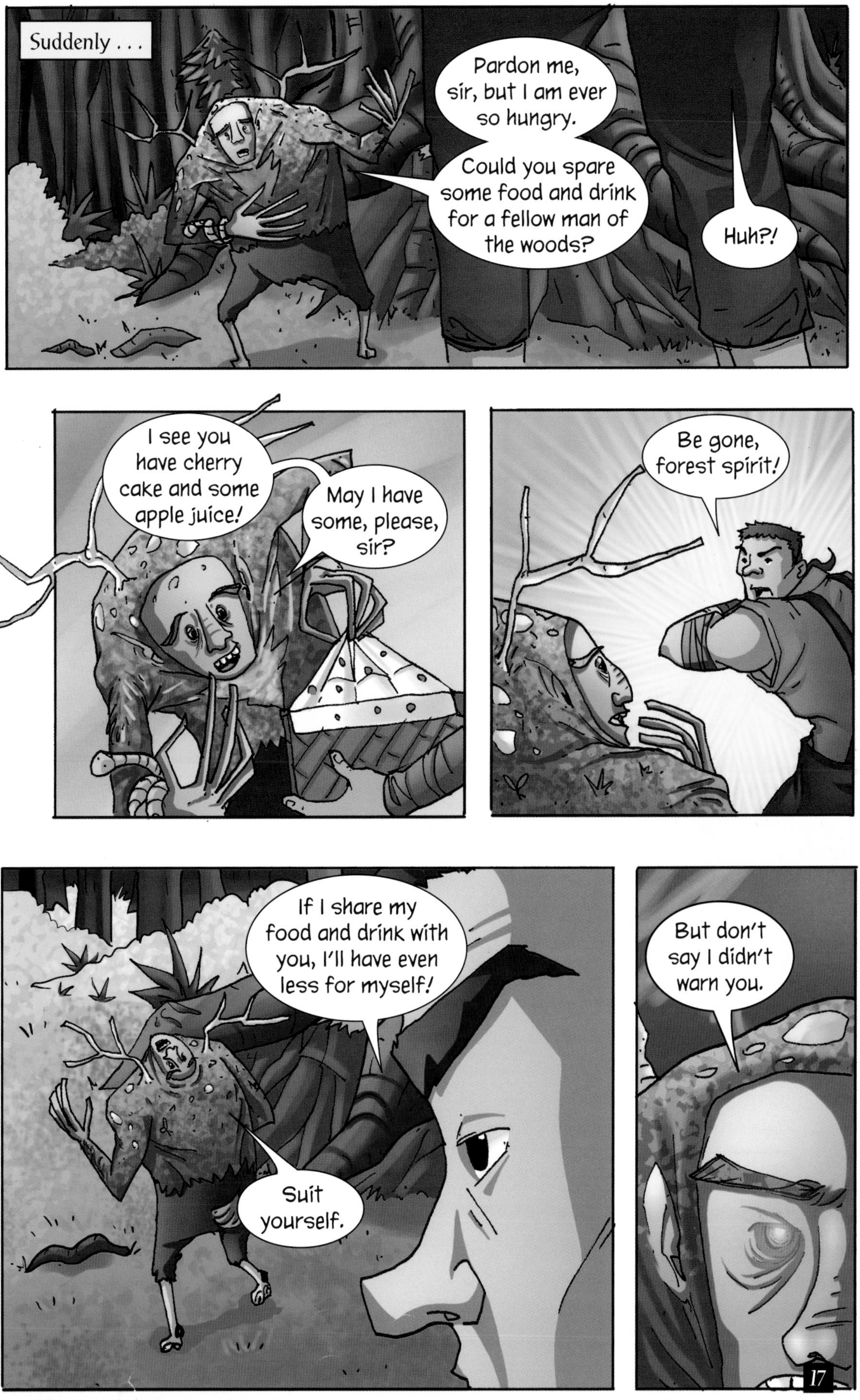
Suddenly . . .
Pardon me, sir, but I am ever so hungry.
Could you spare some food and drink for a fellow man of the woods?
Huh?!
I see you have cherry cake and some apple juice!
May I have some, please, sir?
Be gone, forest spirit!
If I share my food and drink with you, I'll have even less for myself!
Suit yourself.
But don't say I didn't warn you.

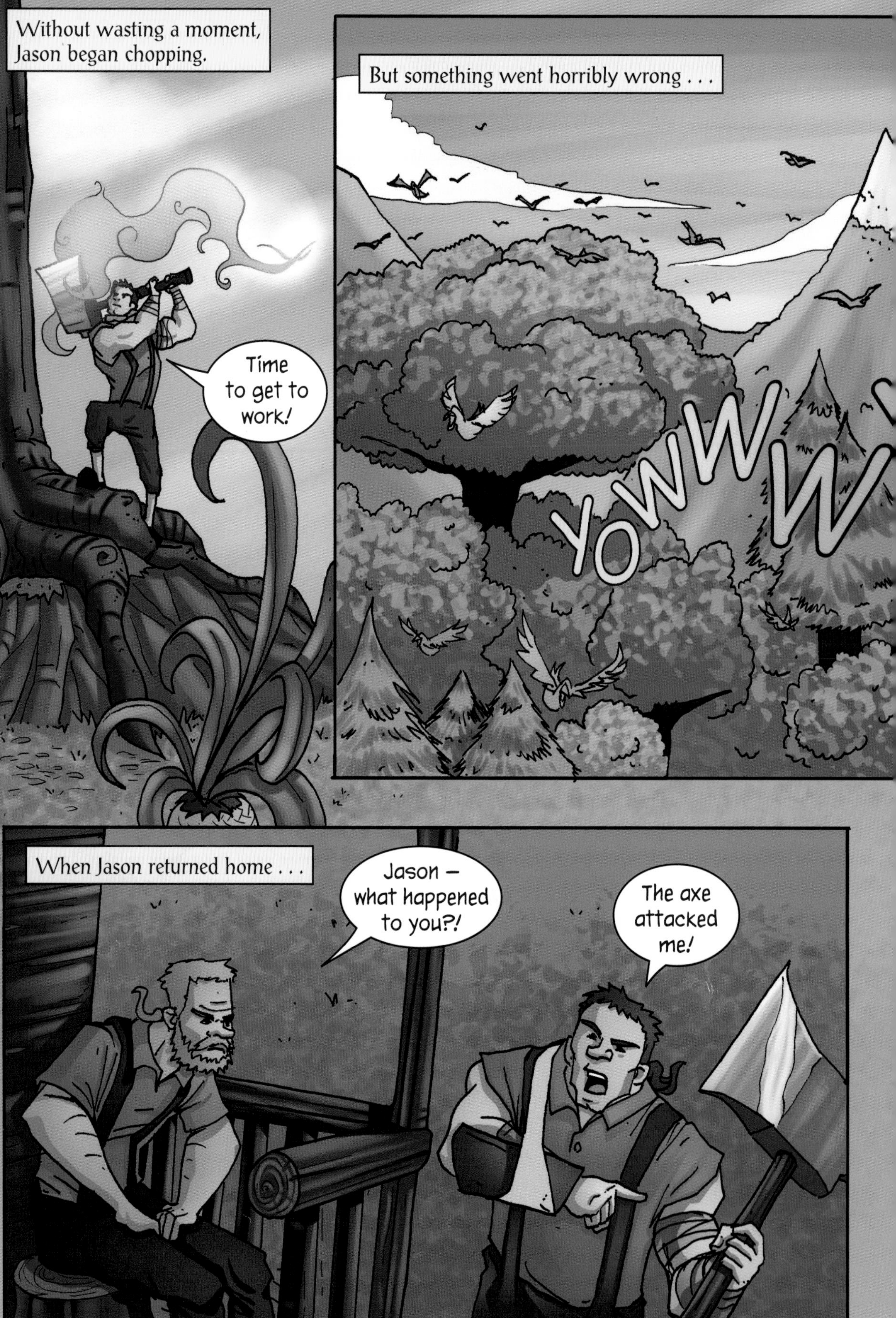
Without wasting a moment, Jason began chopping.
Time to get to work!
But something went horribly wrong . . .
YOWWW
When Jason returned home . . .
Jason — what happened to you?!
The axe attacked me!

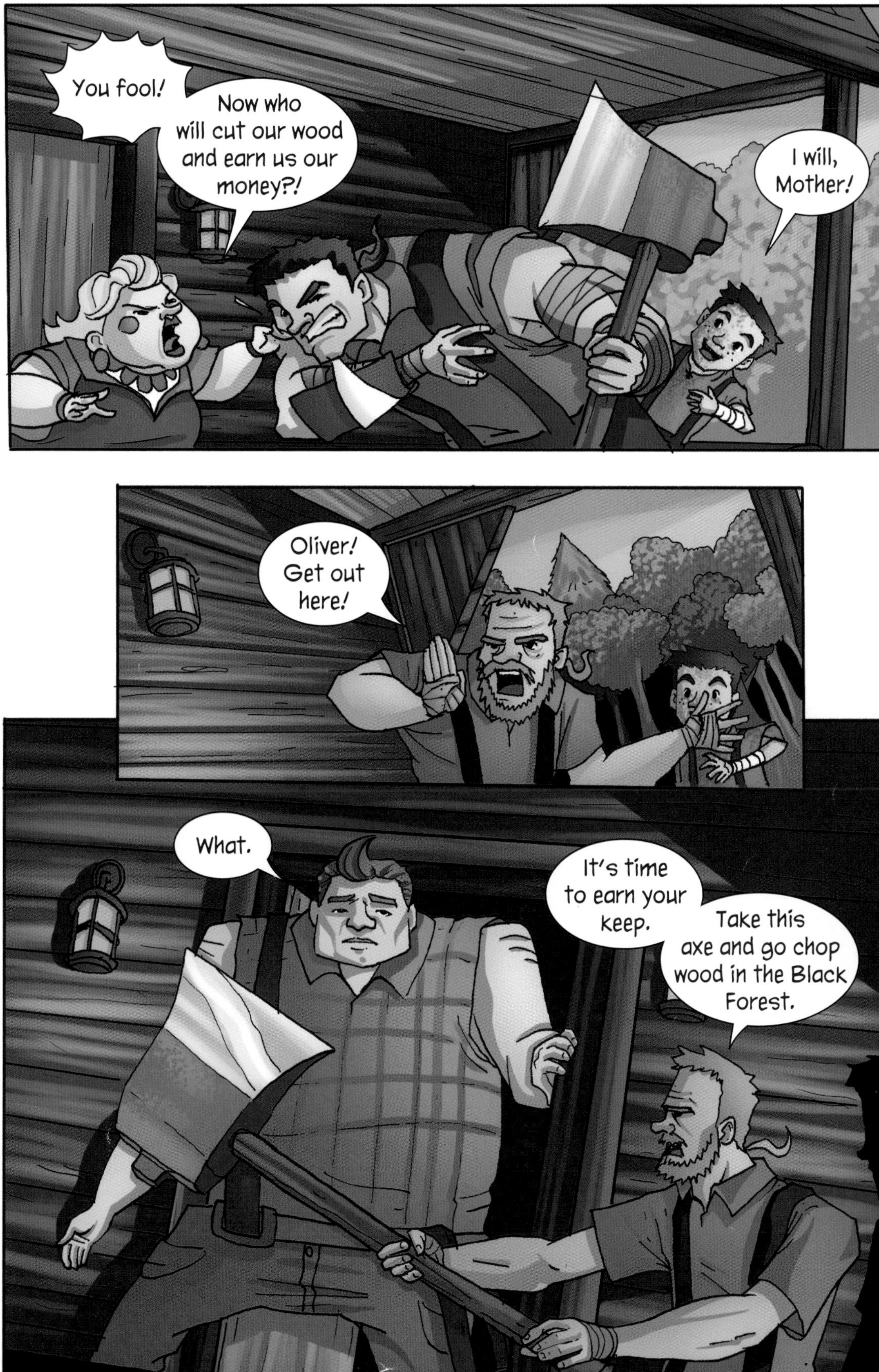
You fool!
Now who will cut our wood and earn us our money?!
I will, Mother!
Oliver! Get out here!
What.
It's time to earn your keep.
Take this axe and go chop wood in the Black Forest.

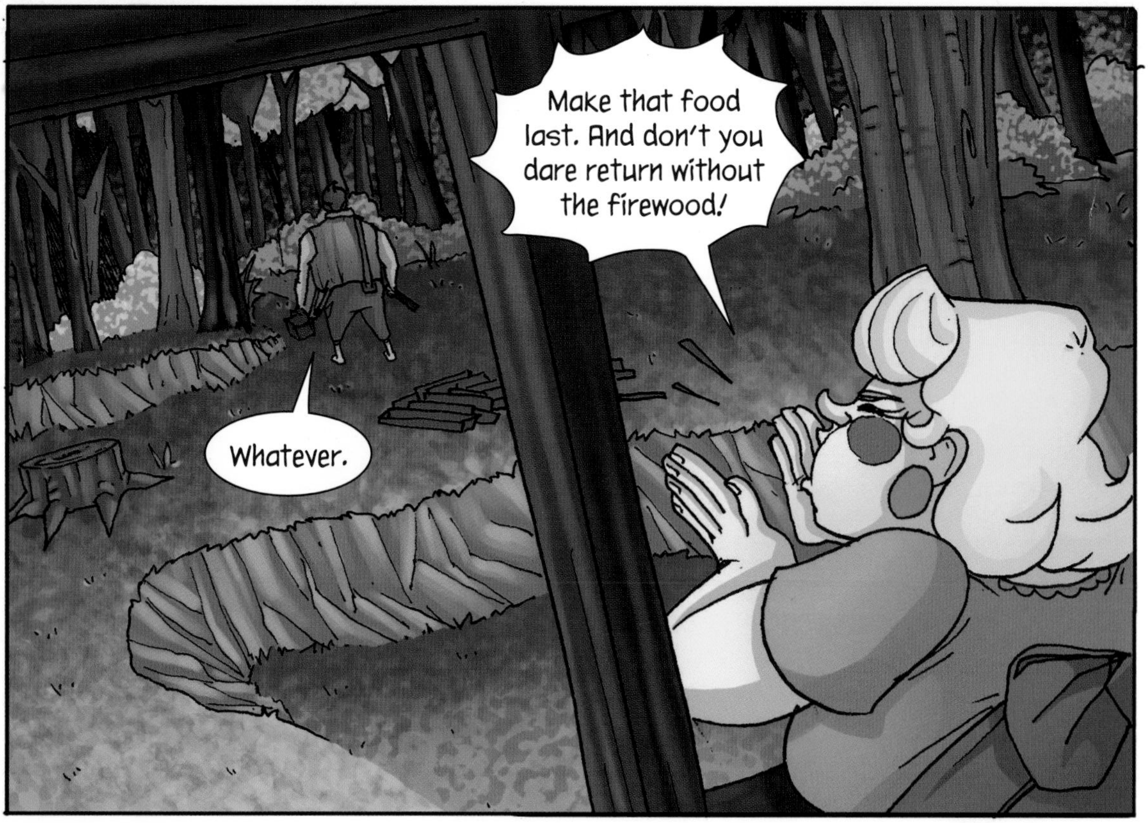
Make that food last. And don't you dare return without the firewood!
Whatever.

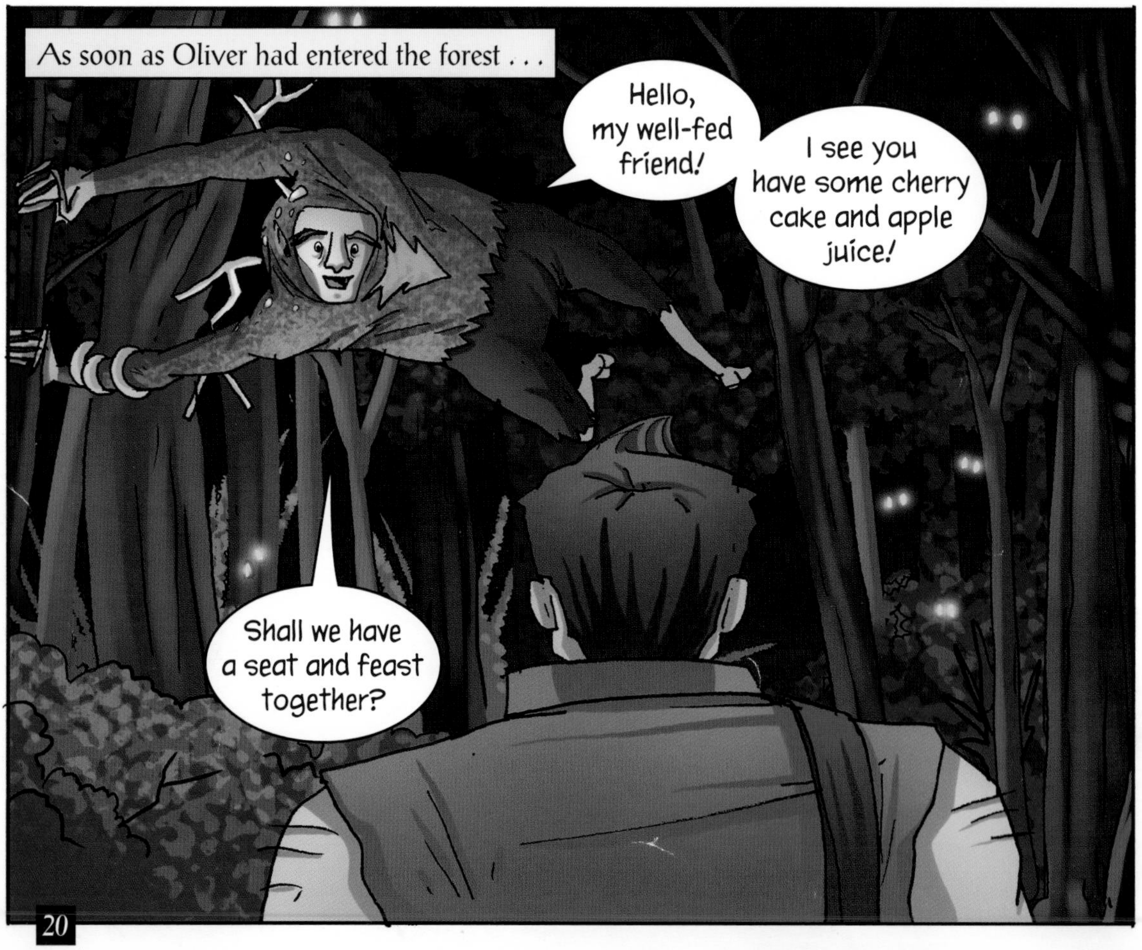
As soon as Oliver had entered the forest . . .
Hello, my well-fed friend!
I see you have some cherry cake and apple juice!
Shall we have a seat and feast together?

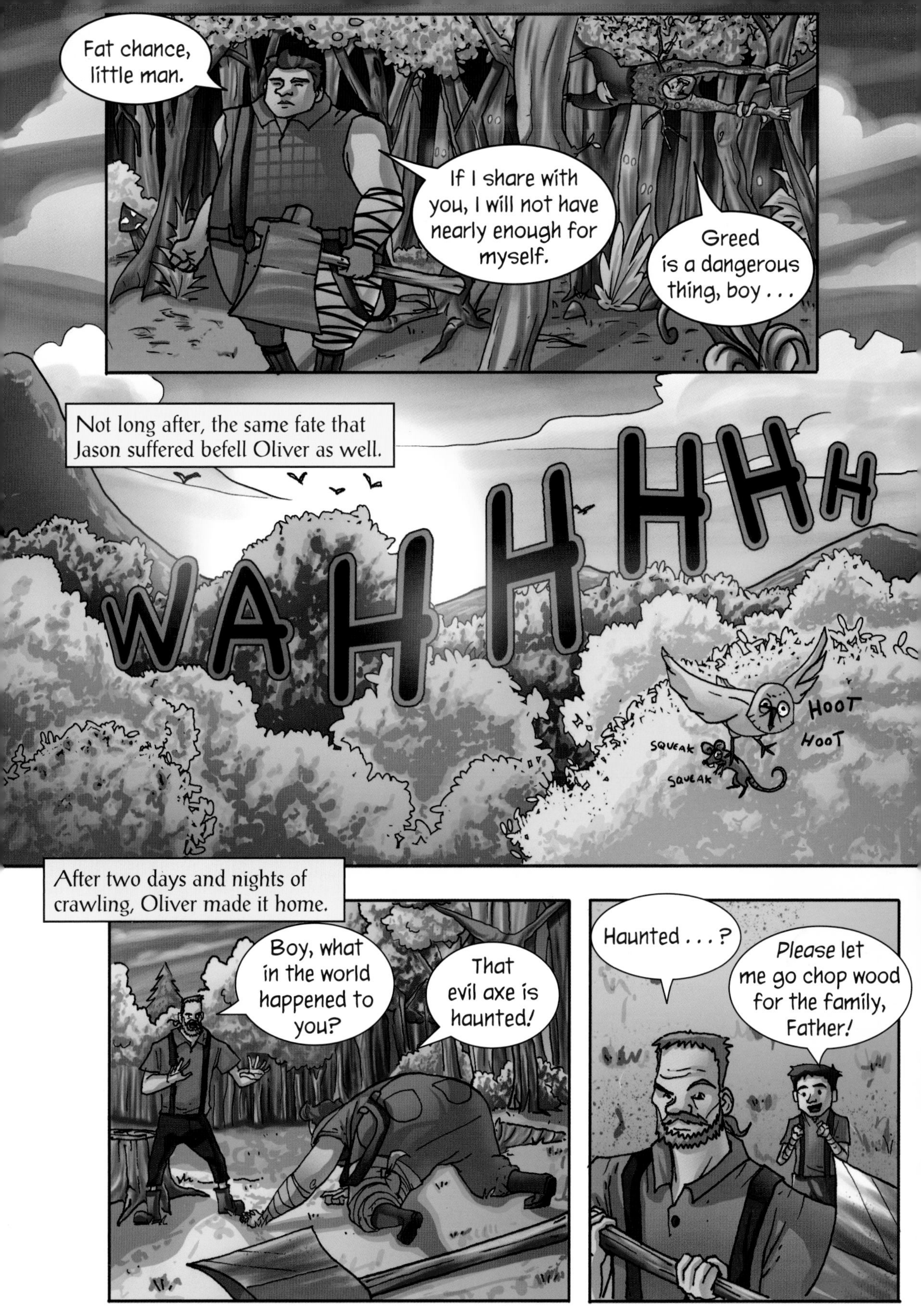
Fat chance, little man.
If I share with you, I will not have nearly enough for myself.
Greed is a dangerous thing, boy . . .
Not long after, the same fate that Jason suffered befell Oliver as well.
WAHHHHHH
HOOT
HOOT
SQUEAK
SQUEAK
After two days and nights of crawling, Oliver made it home.
Boy, what in the world happened to you?
That evil axe is haunted!
Haunted . . . ?
Please let me go chop wood for the family, Father!

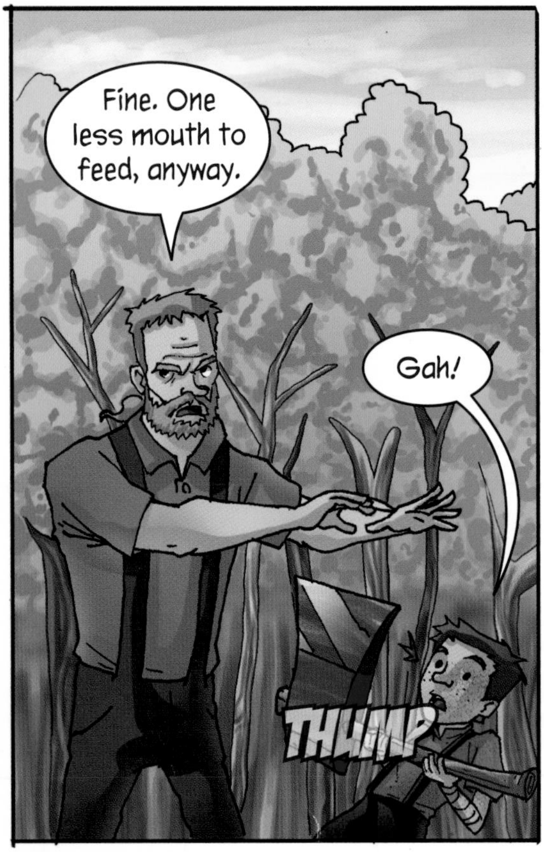
Fine. One less mouth to feed, anyway.
Gah!
THUMP

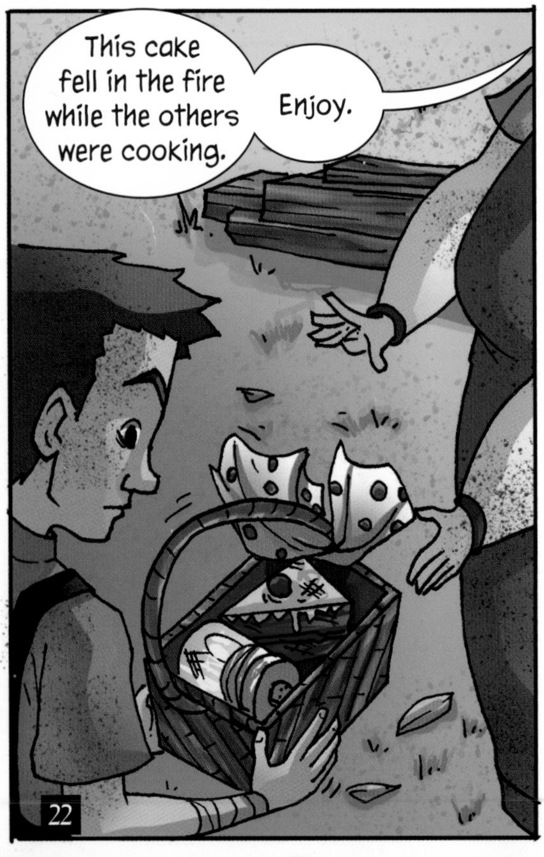
This cake fell in the fire while the others were cooking.
Enjoy.

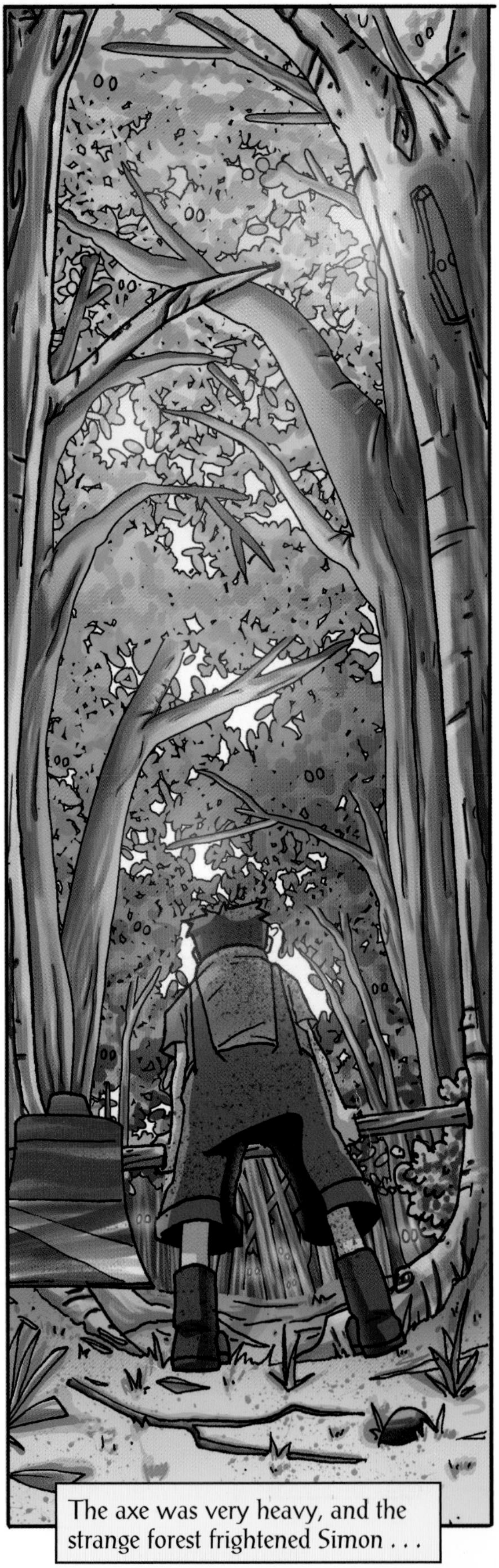
The axe was very heavy, and the strange forest frightened Simon . . .

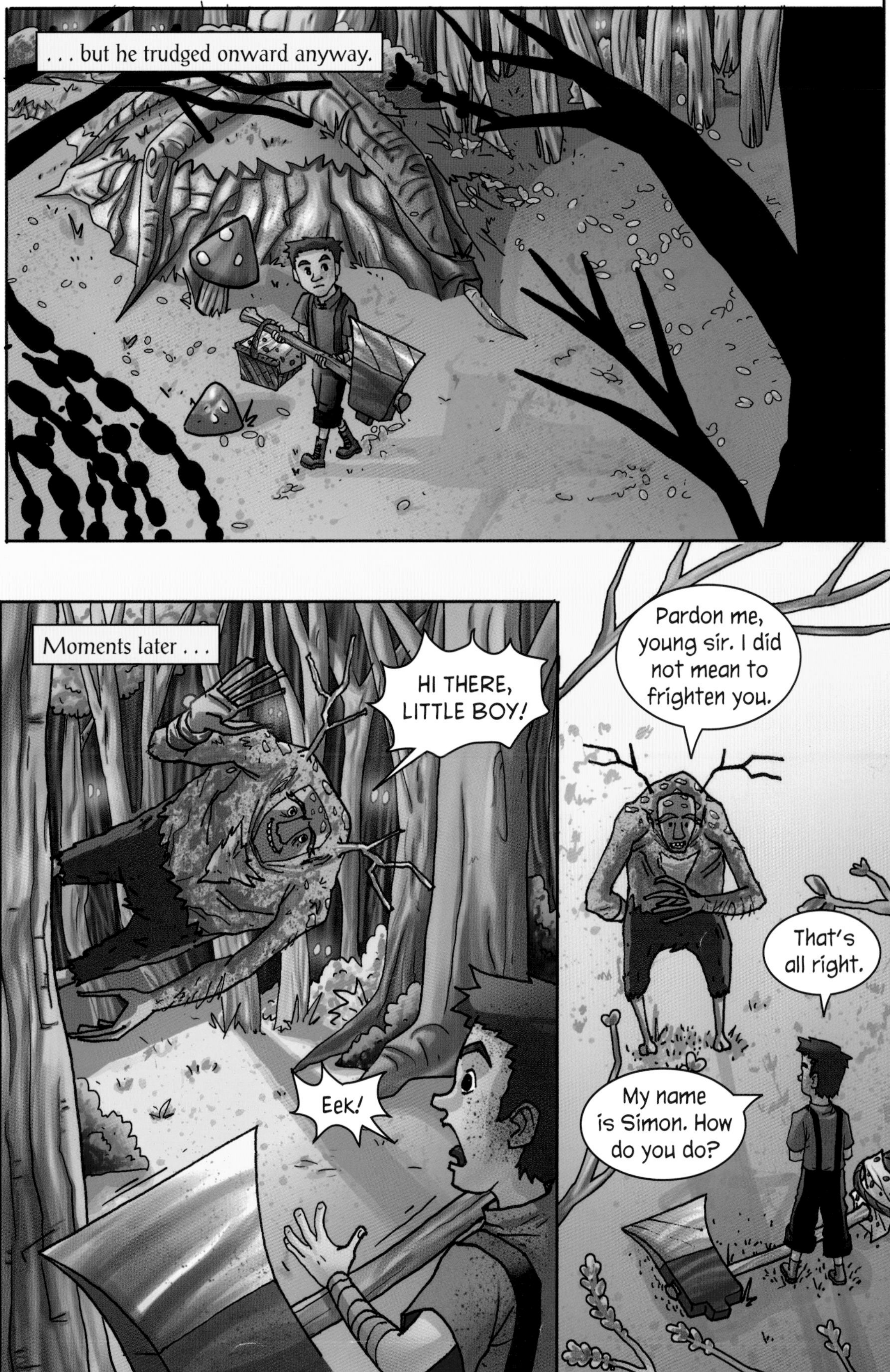
. . . but he trudged onward anyway.
Moments later . . .
HI THERE, LITTLE BOY!
Eek!
Pardon me, young sir. I did not mean to frighten you.
That's all right.
My name is Simon. How do you do?

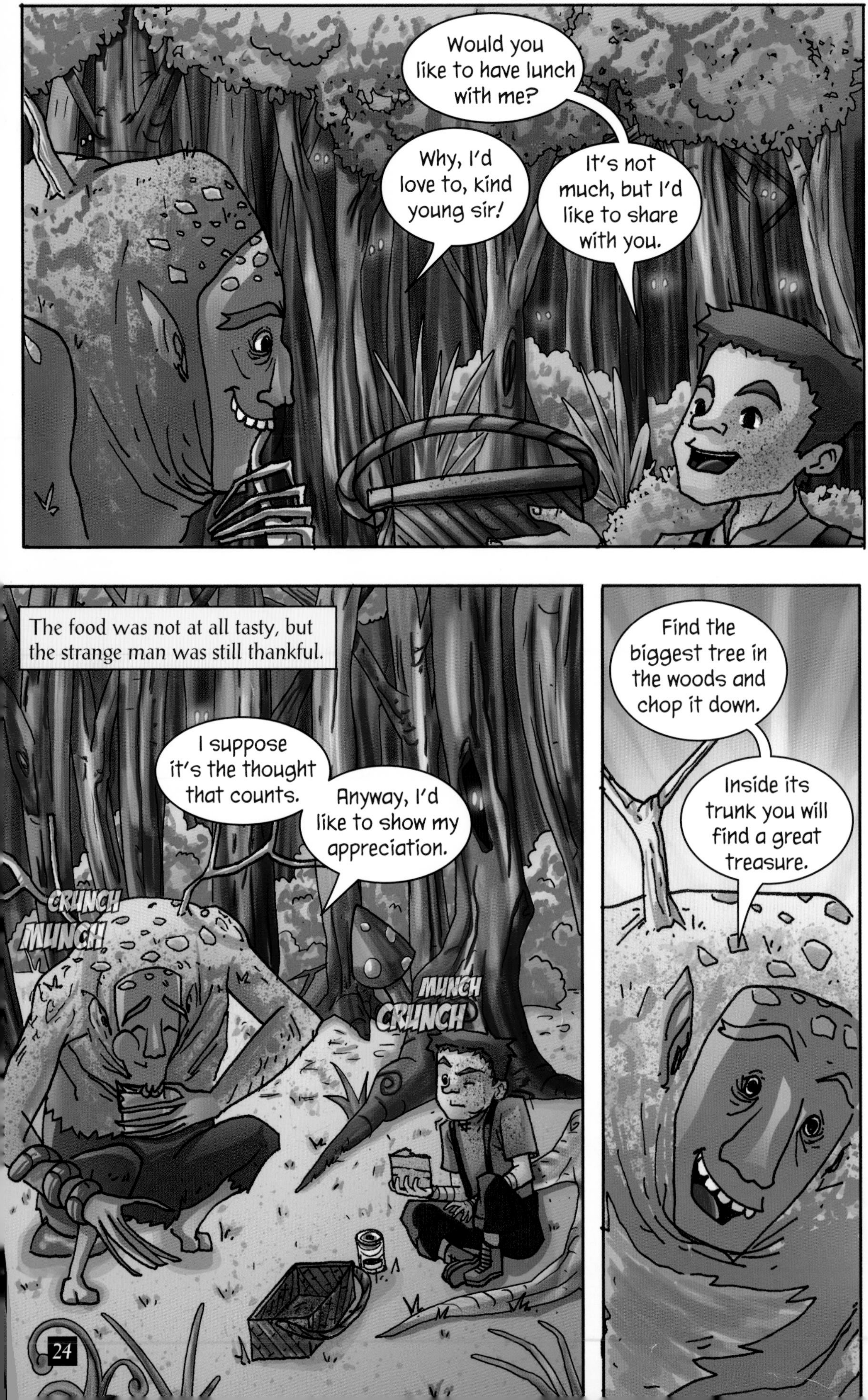

Would you like to have lunch with me?
It's not much, but I'd like to share with you.
Why, I'd love to, kind young sir!
The food was not at all tasty, but the strange man was still thankful.
CRUNCH
MUNCH
MUNCH
CRUNCH
I suppose it's the thought that counts.
Anyway, I'd like to show my appreciation.
Find the biggest tree in the woods and chop it down.
Inside its trunk you will find a great treasure.

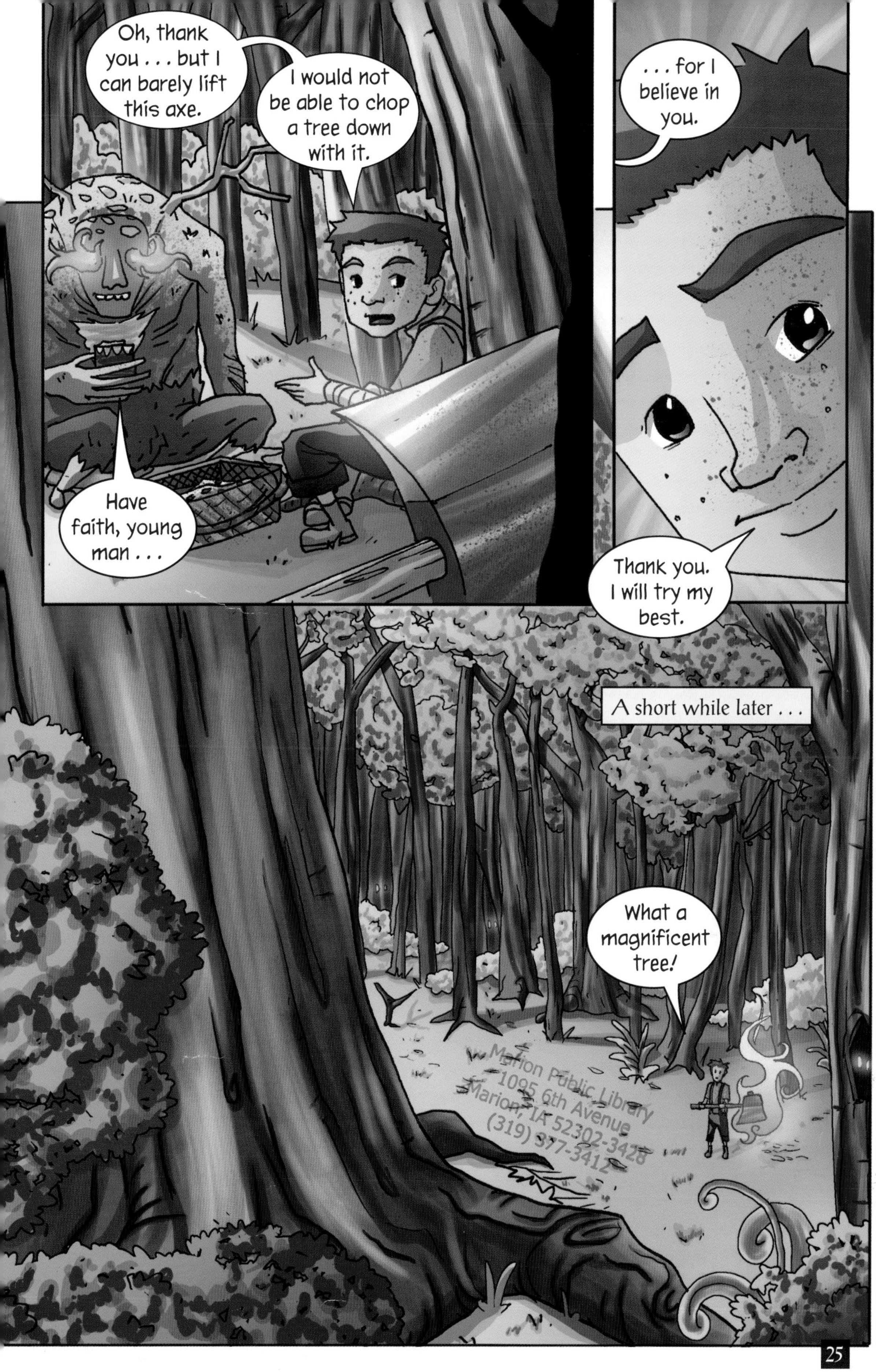
Oh, thank you . . . but I can barely lift this axe.
I would not be able to chop a tree down with it.
Have faith, young man . . .
. . . for I believe in you.
Thank you. I will try my best.
A short while later . . .
What a magnificent tree!

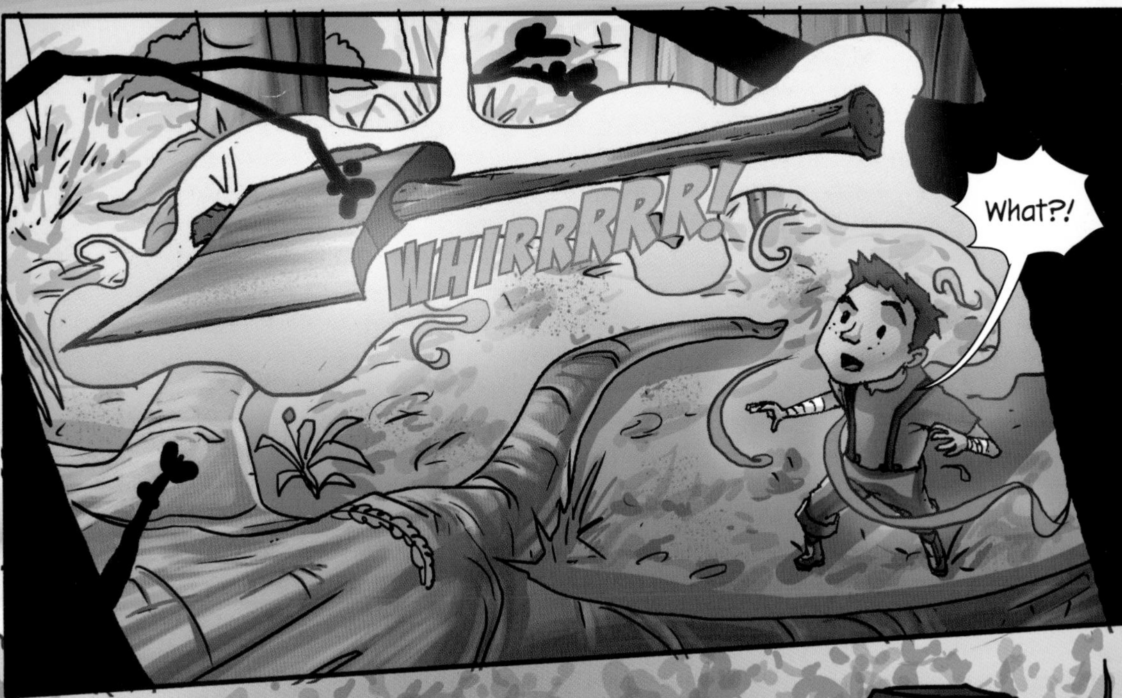
WHIRRRRR!
What?!

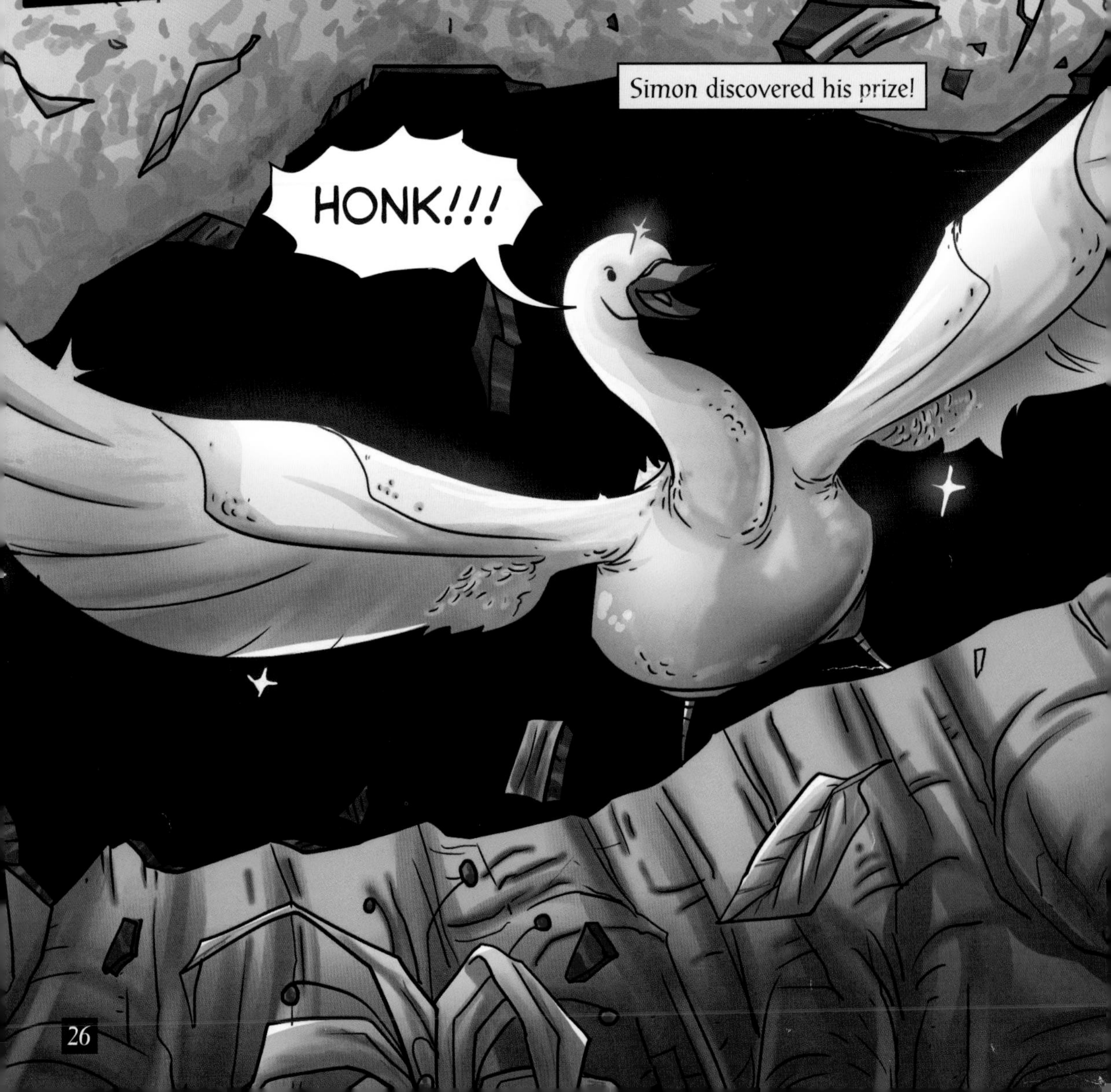
Simon discovered his prize!
HONK!!!

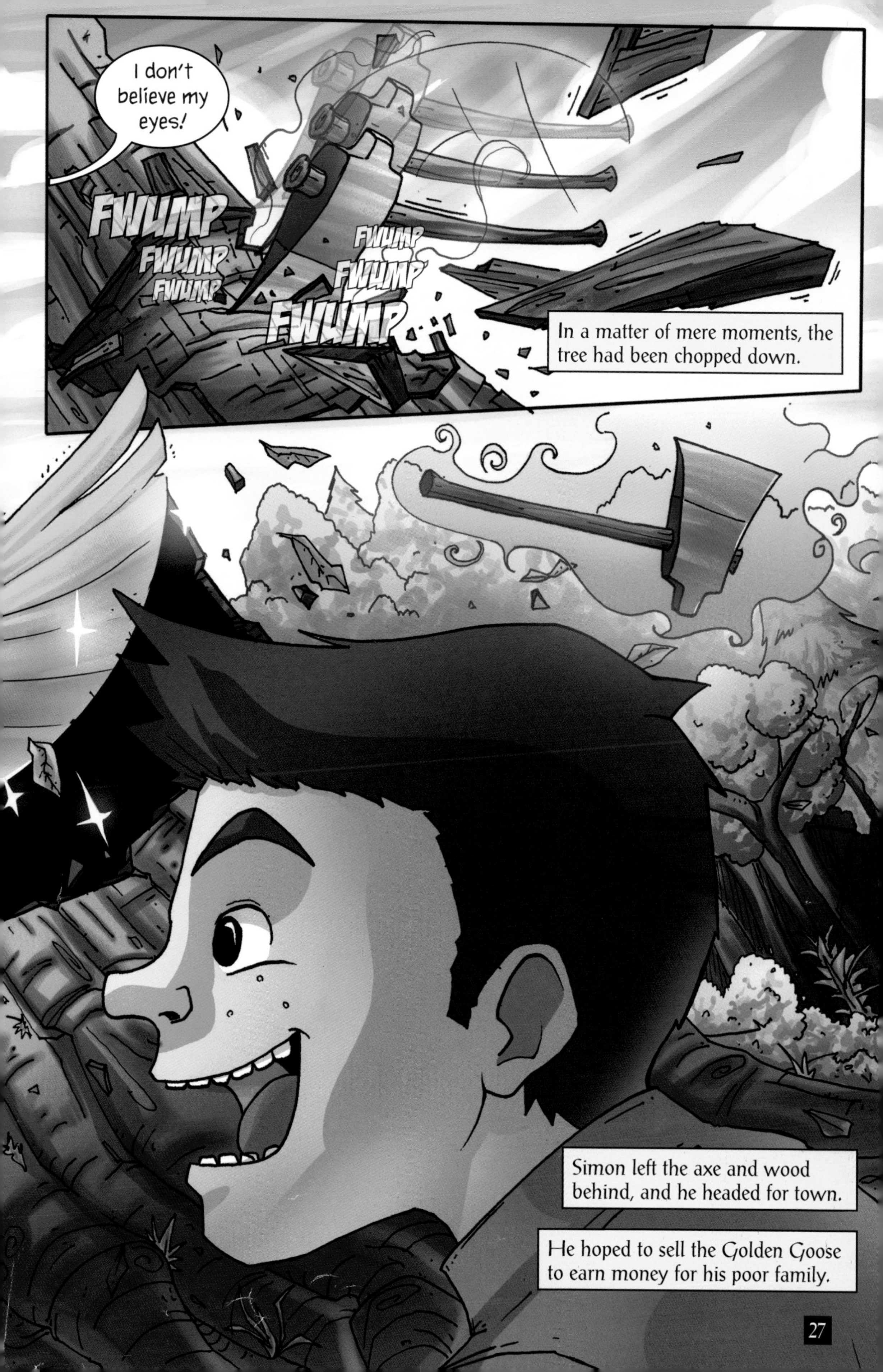
I don't believe my eyes!
FWUMP
FWUMP
FWUMP
FWUMP
FWUMP
FWUMP
In a matter of mere moments, the tree had been chopped down.
Simon left the axe and wood behind, and he headed for town.
He hoped to sell the Golden Goose to earn money for his poor family.

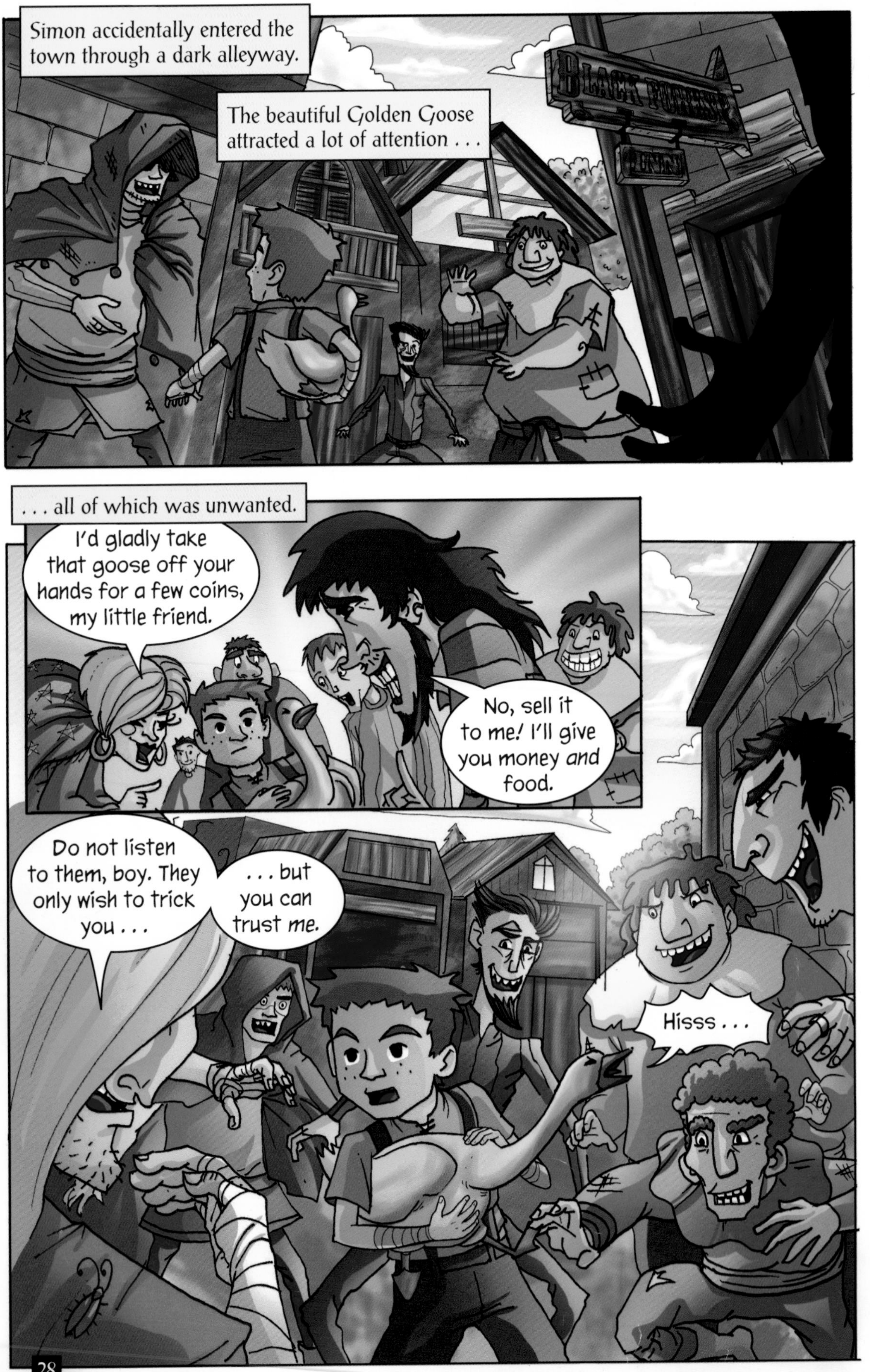
Simon accidentally entered the town through a dark alleyway.
The beautiful Golden Goose attracted a lot of attention . . .
. . . all of which was unwanted.
I'd gladly take that goose off your hands for a few coins, my little friend.
No, sell it to me! I'll give you money and food.
Do not listen to them, boy. They only wish to trick you . . .
. . . but you can trust me.
Hisss . . .

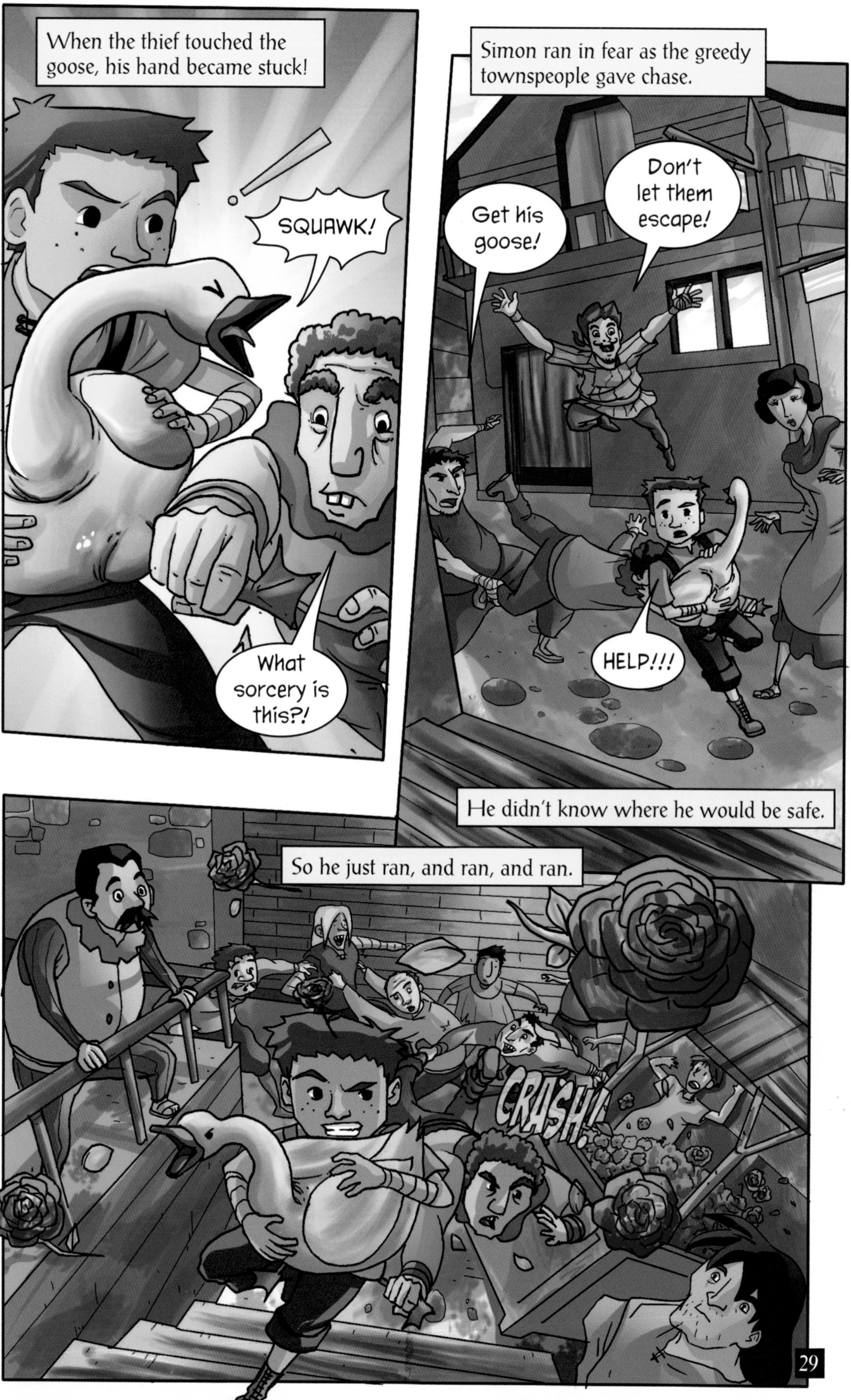
When the thief touched the goose, his hand became stuck!
!
SQUAWK!
What sorcery is this?!
Simon ran in fear as the greedy townspeople gave chase.
Get his goose!
Don't let them escape!
HELP!!!
He didn't know where he would be safe.
So he just ran, and ran, and ran.
CRASH!

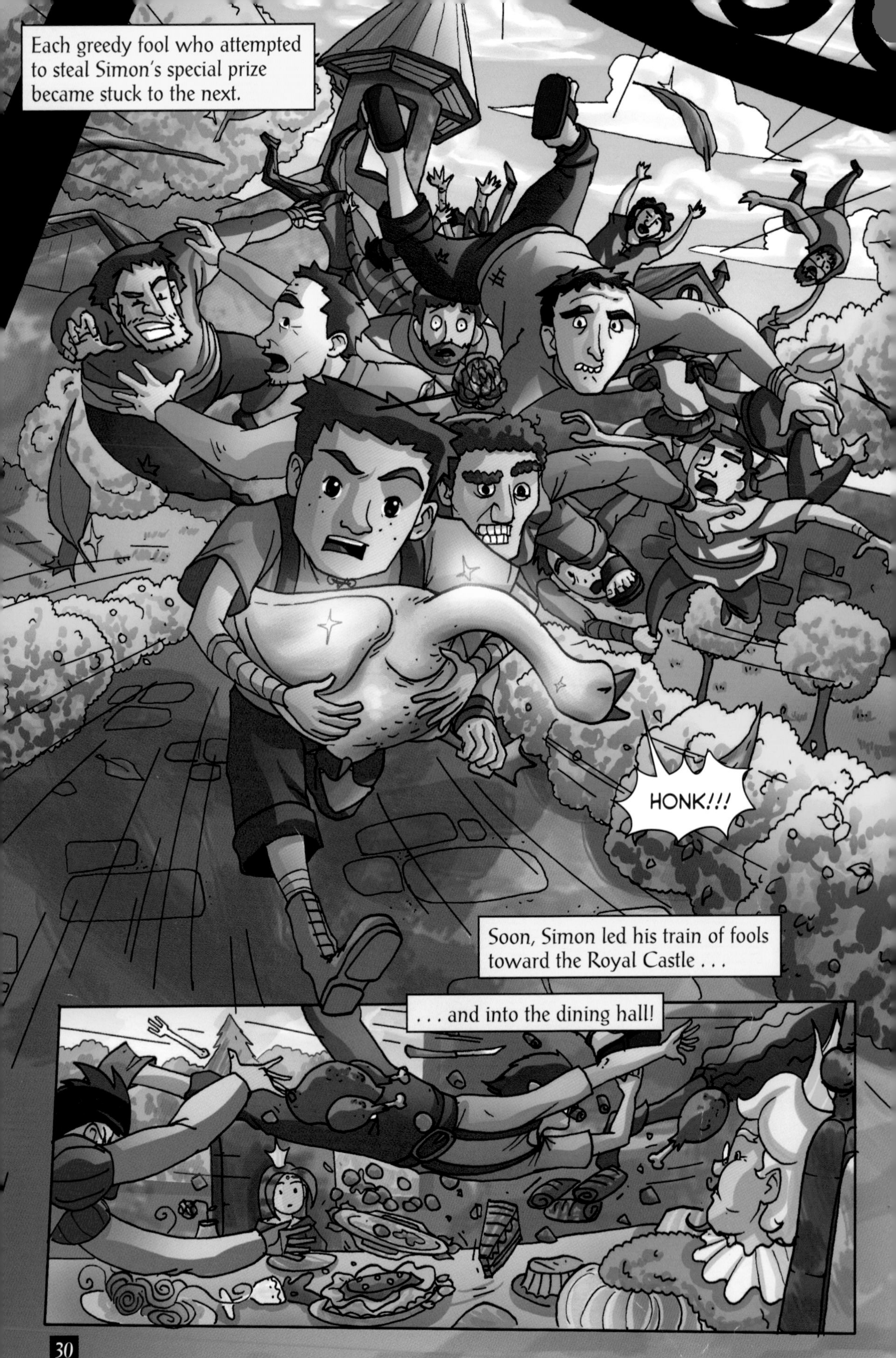
Each greedy fool who attempted to steal Simon's special prize became stuck to the next.
HONK!!!
Soon, Simon led his train of fools toward the Royal Castle . . .
. . . and into the dining hall!

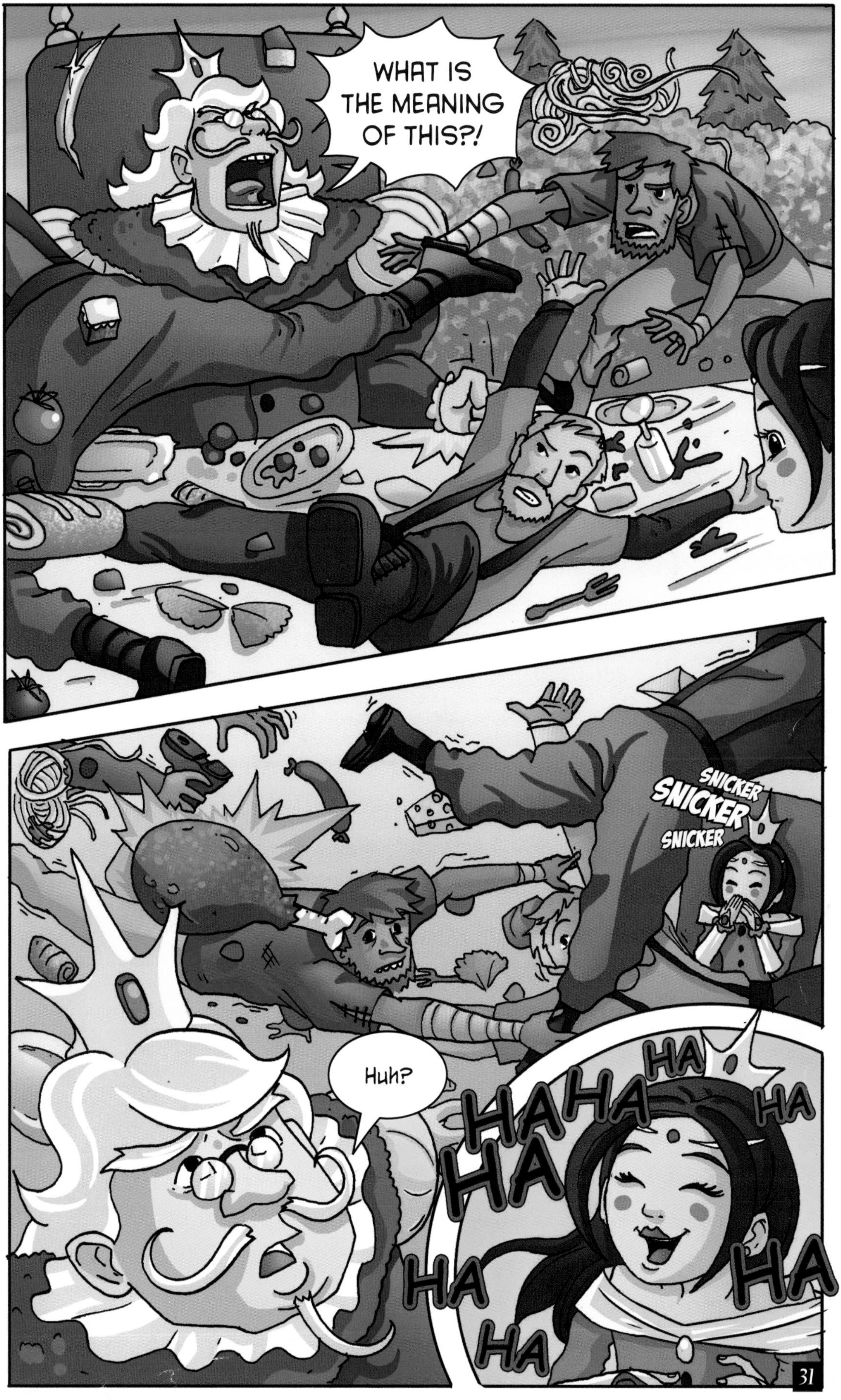
WHAT IS THE MEANING OF THIS?!
SNICKER
SNICKER
SNICKER
Huh?
HA
HAHA
HA
HA
HA
HA
HA
HA

Suddenly, everyone burst into laughter.

HA HA HA HA HA HA HA
HA HA HA HA HA
HA HA HA HA HA
HA HA HA HA HA HA
HA HA HA
HA HA

As laughter filled the halls, the Golden Goose released its hold over the people.

POOF!

It was then that Simon first noticed Princess Eliza.

Simon did not know it, but earlier that day, the King had made a decree.

Any young man who could make the princess laugh would become prince . . .

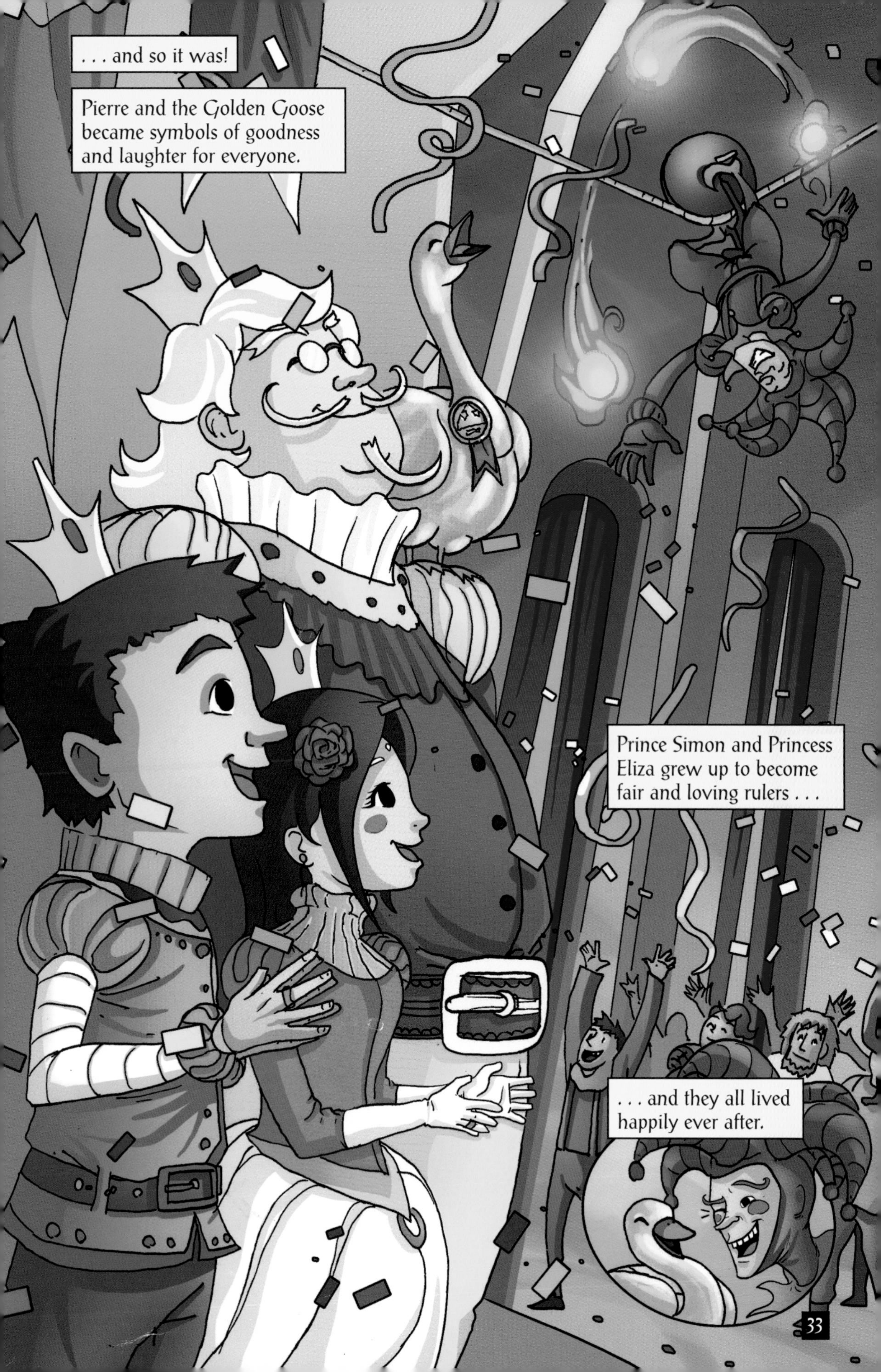
. . . and so it was!
Pierre and the Golden Goose became symbols of goodness and laughter for everyone.
Prince Simon and Princess Eliza grew up to become fair and loving rulers . . .
. . . and they all lived happily ever after.

# THE BROTHERS GRIMM

### *A Family of Folk and Fairy Tales*

Jacob and Wilhelm Grimm were German brothers who invited storytellers to their home so they could write down their tales.

Peasants and villagers, middle-class citizens, wealthy aristocrats — even the Grimms' servants — contributed to their diverse collection of stories!

The brothers also collected folk tales from published works from other cultures and languages, adding to the variety of their sources.

In 1812, the Grimms published their collection of fairy tales, called Children's and Household Tales. The Brothers Grimm were among the first to collect and publish folk and fairy tales taken directly from the people who told them. These days, it would be hard to find anyone who hasn't at least heard of one of the Grimm Brothers' colorful characters!

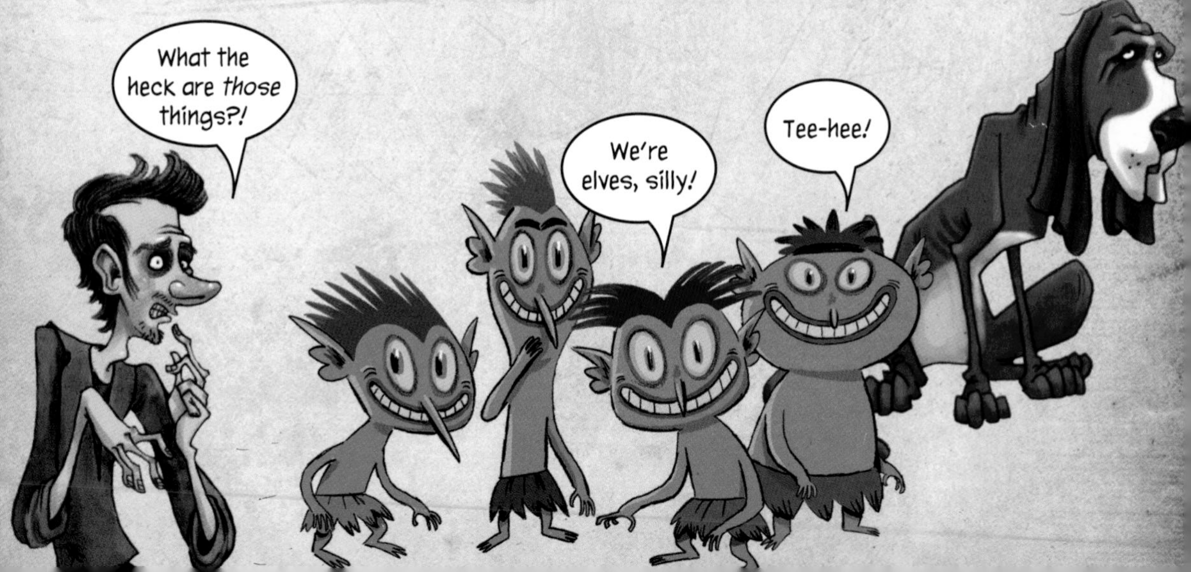
What the heck are *those* things?!
We're elves, silly!
Tee-hee!

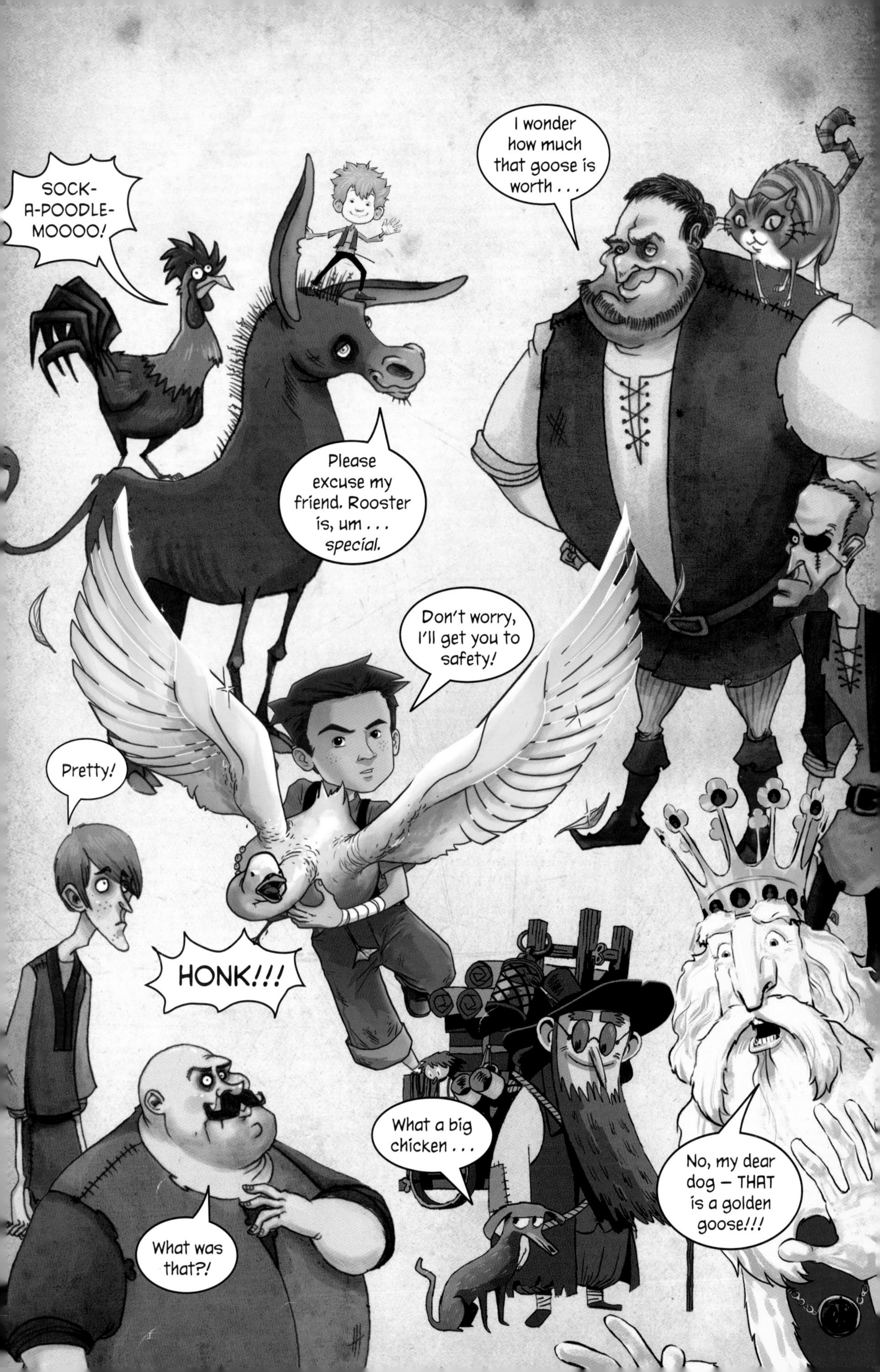
SOCK-A-POODLE-MOOOO!
I wonder how much that goose is worth . . .
Please excuse my friend. Rooster is, um . . . *special.*
Don't worry, I'll get you to safety!
Pretty!
HONK!!!
What a big chicken . . .
No, my dear dog — THAT is a golden goose!!!
What was that?!

# GRIMM GRAPHIC NOVEL...

Travel with *The Bremen Town Musicians*

## About the Retelling Author

Sean Tulien is, in fact, frightened by geese — especially the hissy ones. He is also a children's book editor living and working in Minnesota. In his spare time, he likes to read, eat sushi, exercise outdoors, chase squirrels, listen to loud music, and write books like this one.

## About the Illustrator

Thiago Ferraz started drawing as a hobby. Later, he enrolled in various illustration classes. Soon after, Thiago started doing freelance illustration work. Now, he's able to draw for a living! Thiago has done instructional illustrations, caricatures, and, of course, lots of comic books. Thiago currently works at a gaming company as a 3D illustrator, which he enjoys. Thiago is very grateful for being able to do what he loves for a living!

# Discussion Questions

**1.** Are any of the characters in this book evil? Which ones do you think are good? Why?

**2.** People try to steal Simon's golden goose. Has anyone tried to take something that was special to you? Talk about it.

**3.** Is Simon a hero? Discuss your opinions.

# Writing Prompts

**1.** The Wild Man helped Simon find the Golden Goose. Why do you think he helped Simon, but not either of Simon's brothers? Explain your answer.

**2.** Who do you think the Wild Man is? Is he a forest spirit? Is he just wearing a disguise? What does he like to do for fun? Write a story about the Wild Man.

**3.** What happens next to Simon and Eliza? Write another story about the adventures of Simon, Eliza, and the Golden Goose. Then turn it into a short graphic novel with illustrations!

# Glossary

*appreciation* (uh-pree-shee-AY-shuhn)—a feeling of thankfulness or gratitude

*befell* (bi-FEL)—happened to someone

*decree* (di-KREE)—an official decision or order

*faith* (FAYTH)—trust and confidence in someone or something

*haunted* (HAWNT-id)—if a place is haunted, then ghosts or evil spirits live there

*jester* (JES-tur)—an entertainer and performer for royalty in the Middle Ages

*magnificent* (mag-NIF-i-sent)—very impressive or beautiful

*runt* (RUNT)—a small or weak person or animal

*spectacular* (spek-TAK-yuh-lur)—remarkable or dramatic

*strange* (STRAYNJ)—different, odd, or unfamiliar

*suffered* (SUHF-urd)—had pain, discomfort, or sorrow

*warn* (WORN)—to give advice in advance

More

# GRIMM BROTHERS GRAPHIC NOVELS

by STONE ARCH BOOKS . . .

A GRIMM GRAPHIC NOVEL
retold by Martin Powell
illustrated by Pedro Rodriguez
THE ELVES and the SHOEMAKER

A GRIMM GRAPHIC NOVEL
THE BREMEN TOWN MUSICIANS
retold by Louise Simonson
illustrated by Lisa Weber

A GRIMM GRAPHIC NOVEL
TOM THUMB

# STILL WANT MORE?

**Find cool websites and more books like this one at www.Facthound.com.**

Just type in the Book ID: **9781434229618** and you're ready to go!

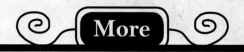

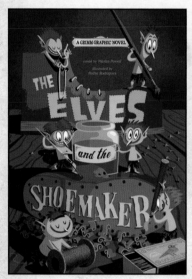

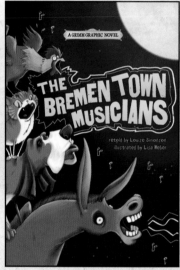

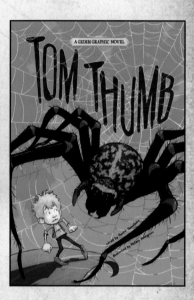